BLADE LAW

A silver necklet was all that was left to identify the body of the man McKee found dead in the mountains. The brutal murder was the work of Juan Darringo and his bandits who had made the mountain ranges their lair of robbery and death . . . However, identification of the dead man was to lead McKee back to the mountains accompanied by a man intent on retribution. Now, forced to pit their wits against the cruel terrain, they also find themselves the prey in a hunt that will have only one outcome.

JACK REASON

BLADE LAW

Complete and Unabridged

LINFORD
Leicester

First published in Great Britain in 2005 by
Robert Hale Limited
London

First Linford Edition
published 2006
by arrangement with
Robert Hale Limited
London

The moral right of the author has been asserted

British Library CIP Data

Reason, Jack
    Blade law.—Large print ed.—
    Linford western library
    1. Western stories
    2. Large type books
    I. Title
    823.9'14 [F]

    ISBN 1–84617–284–5

Published by
F. A. Thorpe (Publishing)
Anstey, Leicestershire

Set by Words & Graphics Ltd.
Anstey, Leicestershire
Printed and bound in Great Britain by
T. J. International Ltd., Padstow, Cornwall

This book is printed on acid-free paper

For J.J.
who will find his own trail
when the time comes

1

He waited for the high drifting hawk to circle the rocks for the third time before easing his mount from the shade. He was certain now. There was a body out there, probably dead, sprawled in the clutter of boulders and dirt at the foot of the sheer-faced peak.

Maybe the fellow had fallen, broken a limb or become trapped, found himself unable to move and finally given in to the torture of the searing heat and blazing sun. Maybe a rattler had struck.

Or maybe he had been shot and robbed. It happened hereabouts in wild country only miles from the southern border. Roaming *bandidos* out of Passo Marie were always on the look-out for easy pickings from those crossing the ranges to the lusher plains beyond.

Single wagons following the main trail, lone riders taking the mountain tracks, the occasional hunter heading West, the ever optimistic prospector, nobody was safe if spotted by the bandits and reckoned vulnerable enough to be attacked, stripped clean of clothes and possessions and left for the hungry hawks.

Could be the bird up there had seen it all, thought the man, tightening his hold on the reins.

He scanned the cloudless sky again, squinting against the glare of the sun. The bird was still there, still drifting, watching and waiting. It might be another half-hour before it swooped lower and risked a closer look. The hawk was in no hurry. Men were a long time dead.

The mount tossed its head and snorted as it picked its way through the loose stones and parched scrub. 'Easy, easy,' murmured the man, his gaze concentrating on the ledge high above the rocks where the hawk had come to rest, one eye on the approaching rider, the other on whatever lay hidden in the rocks.

The man loosened the reins through

his fingers and urged the mount on, his shadow thrusting across the sheer face like a suddenly stalking monster. The hawk screeched and spread its wings menacingly, the horse snorted again and clipped its hoofs defiantly through the dirt.

'Easy,' urged the man, reining the mount towards the deeper shade at a cluster of boulders. He dismounted, wiped the sticky sweat from his neck and climbed into the rocks.

It was unlikely someone had ridden into this maze, he pondered, scrambling through the clefts and over craggy surfaces. A horse would never have made it; a man would have needed one hell of a reason for trying. Or one hell of a threat to run from. He shielded his eyes to gaze at the staring bird, cursed quietly beneath his breath and climbed on.

The hawk screeched angrily again. The man spat and watched his dripping sweat stain the rock surfaces and spread like blots. He had no good reason to be doing this, he thought, no darned reason at all. He could have stayed with the main trail, cleared the mountains and made it to the plains in less than two days. He had been intent on doing just that when the hawk had drifted to its mournful circling. No mistaking then the ominous signs, and no turning his back on them either.

He fixed the bird's stare resentfully for a moment and reached for the next safe hand-hold. Maybe there was somebody out here in need of help. Maybe there was a fellow simply waiting, hoping, praying. But silently.

The man grunted. Or maybe the hawk knew a whole sight more.

★ ★ ★

He had been dead since before nightfall, the man reckoned. Stripped to his vest and johns, hands roped behind him, then shot in the back of the head. One shot. An execution.

The man glanced quickly at the still

staring hawk, its glare watching his every movement, its neck craned forward, body tensed. 'Hell,' he murmured, blinking on the sight of the twisted shape tumbled among the rocks. Youngish fellow, he thought, somewhere in his middle twenties; light-haired, fine features, neat, clean hands. No drifter, not a man of the land with hands like that; maybe a town man, storekeeper, bank clerk, somebody privileged, familiar with life's comforts.

So what in tarnation had brought him to this godforsaken wilderness? Where had he come from? Where had he been heading, and why? A deal more to the point, who had shot him?

No guesses needed as to who. The young man had almost certainly died at the hands of *bandidos* out of Passo Marie. The killing had all their marks: robbed of possessions, including the fellow's mount, stripped down to the last stitch of clothing, then murdered in cold blood. It would have been all over in twenty minutes with the *bandidos* fading into the mountains again like shadows.

Only one thing for it now, thought the man, bury the young fellow decent and out of the reach of the hungry hawk and the scavenging buzzards and vultures that would surely follow, then pick up the main trail and head for the plains. Nothing more to be done here. What he had found was more than enough.

He wiped the sweat from his face and neck, gave the bird a withering look and eased himself carefully towards the body.

But he had gone only a few stumbling steps when the voice cracked and echoed from somewhere high above him.

'Hey, gringo, that fella your partner or somebody? You riding along of him?' The voice wheezed into laughter. 'I hope not for your sake, eh? Otherwise I might have to kill you too, but seeing as I'm going to do that anyhow, what the hell!'

2

The thickly stubbled, dark-skinned *bandido*, with bright, piercing eyes, wet lips and a cynically lopsided grin creasing his face, stood alone in the sunbaked rocks.

A dusty, battered sombrero hung loose at his back, a bandoleer gleamed across his chest. The glinting barrel of a Winchester lay easy in his grip, while a hefty paunch rolled over his belted trousers and the polished butt of a high holstered Colt.

'Hey, gringo,' he called again, the grin collapsing, 'you got ears? I'm speaking to you. You got a voice?'

'I hear you,' answered the man, his gaze moving swiftly but intently over the surrounding rocks for a sight of the *bandido*'s sidekicks.

'Well, I am pleased to hear that, my friend. Pleased to hear that Juan

Darringo is not wasting his breath.' The grin creased into life again. 'You heard of me, gringo? You know the name of Darringo?'

'Can't say I do,' croaked the man, still scanning the rocks for a telltale movement, the glint of a barrel, shift of a shadow.

'No, not heard of Darringo?' mocked the *bandido*. 'Then this must be your lucky day, eh? How about that, gringo? You get to meeting the famous Juan Darringo, then get shot by him, all in one day! I call that a privilege.' Darringo freshened his grip on the rifle. 'But you haven't answered my question. Do you know the dead man?'

'Never set eyes on him before.'

Darringo licked his lips as the piercing eyes fixed the man in a steady stare. 'So,' he began slowly, 'you too are travelling alone, eh? We have been watching you, my friend. Very carefully.' The grin broadened to a glistening smile across stained yellow teeth.

The man's gaze shifted back to the

bandido. He had said 'we'. How many, he wondered, and where? In the higher rocks, or lower, maybe right here only yards from the dead body.

The hawk stretched its wings but remained perched. The heat shimmered. The air seemed to thicken.

'It is a sad pity,' mocked Darringo, loosening the smile to a wet-lipped pout. 'All these people travelling alone. Is it any wonder they get to being killed? Ain't that so, gringo? You agree, eh?'

'You shoot this young fella?' asked the man, adding as much of an edge to his voice as he could summon. 'Back of the head with his hands tied. That ain't no shootin'. That's murder.'

'Murder, eh?' sneered Darringo. He spat noisily into the rocks at his feet. 'You call it murder. But it makes no difference to Darringo, my friend. A man dead is a man dead. Who cares how he got to being dead? Darringo don't.' His smile broadened again. 'You agree, gringo? Surely you see that.'

What now, wondered the man, his gaze squinting in the relentless glare, the sweat trickling softly down his spine? How much longer before Darringo loosed a shot, or had his sidekicks move in to rope their new find like a lame steer? He eased a hand slowly to clear the beading across his lips, tasted the bitter salt, swallowed and shifted his weight from one foot to the other.

'Tell me, gringo,' called Darringo, 'how come you do not pack a gun? No sidearm, no holster, no rifle. What's with that, eh? Sharp-looking gringo like you shouldn't be so foolish. So what's with you? You got some angel sitting on your shoulder or something? Or maybe you've got some piece hidden some place, eh? That the way of it, gringo? You holding out on Darringo?'

'That's for me to know and you to find out.'

The man had tensed in his clipped retort, his stare suddenly sharper, concentrated, watchful of Darringo's slightest movement, the merest shift of his stance. And there was still nothing, not a hint, of the *bandido*'s sidekicks. But they had to be there, damnit.

'Hey, you're getting big-mouthed there, gringo. Darringo don't like that. No, no . . . *I do not like*. You will pay for the lip, eh? Sure you will.' Darringo gestured to left and right, his glinting gaze flicking like a light into the maze of rocks and boulders. 'I call the shots here, gringo. Don't you go forgetting it.'

The man heard the ominous click of rifle bolts as weapons were primed and levelled. One, two, three — sidekicks still hidden, waiting on the order to shoot. Or would it be another execution?

'I advise you not to move, my friend,' smiled Darringo, relaxing again. 'My compatriots get jumpy at the slightest movement.' He wiped a hand across the stubble. 'So, tell me, gringo, what's your name, where you come from, why you travelling alone up here, where you heading? You going to tell me before I kill you?'

The sweat on the man's brow thickened and grew colder. 'No, I reckon I'll take the personal details to my grave. They ain't no business of yours, anyhow.'

Darringo shrugged, spat, and gestured again with the rifle. 'Suit yourself. A name dies with its owner. It is of no value.'

Shadows moved in the rocks. A trickle of pebbles echoed eerily. A shape grew on the light ahead of the man; a skinny-limbed, loose-lipped *bandido* clutching a gleaming rifle, his fingers already itchy, his eyes anxious. The man did not move, conscious now of a second shape materializing to his left, the scrape of a boot on rock to his right.

He glanced quickly at the glaring hawk, nodded to Darringo as if in acknowledgement of being surrounded, outnumbered and outgunned, then, without so much as an intake of breath, flashed a hand to the back of his neck.

The concealed knife was in the man's grip and cutting air in its deadly aim in seconds. The loose-lipped *bandido* fell back, his eyes wide, mouth open on a deep groan as the blade buried itself deep in his neck.

'Shift!' hissed the man to himself, flinging himself headlong to the left, rolling to the cover of a bulging boulder under a hail of gunfire from Darringo and his remaining sidekicks.

The man gasped, choking on a surge of breath, wiped the sweat from his face and reached into the top of his boot for a second knife that glinted like a shaft of silver in his hand. He swallowed, waited. The *bandido* to his left fired a wild shot in the echo of a string of curses and orders from Darringo still straddling the higher rocks, and came towards the boulders.

He had come to within a step of the bulk's shadow when the man's second blade flashed across the light and thudded into his chest.

'Hey, sonofa-gringo-bitch, what the hell you doing taking out my boys like that?' yelled Darringo blazing another wild shot high into the clear blue sky. 'For that, you die twice, eh? Once, to bring the pain but keep you breathing; twice, as slow as we can make it.' He cursed, issued an order in Spanish and levelled the barrel of the rifle. 'Now!'

The third sidekick stepped into the full glare of the sun. His eyes were dark and narrowed to tight, concentrated slits as he approached the man's cover in the boulders.

'Be very careful, gringo,' snarled Darringo from the ledge. 'Pedro there is not a patient man, but he will shoot you most carefully if you get to being foolish.'

The man licked his lips; his right hand slid slowly to the inside of his shirt. There would be only one chance, he resolved, his fingers folding gently on the handle of the blade strapped across his chest. Just one . . .

The hawk screamed, spread its vast wings and clattered noisily from the crags, swooping low over Darringo's head.

The sidekick broke his concentration; the blade flashed; Darringo began to lose his balance and toppled backwards and, for a crazed minute, the air was filled with echoing curses, the gurgling groans of the third sidekick in his death throes, and the screams of a wheeling hawk.

And when the silence settled again the man moved from the boulders like a breathing shadow.

3

It was another full minute, with the hawk circling soundlessly now to cast its shadow like a shifting shroud across the rocks, before the man crept to the bodies of the sidekicks.

He removed the knives carefully, clinically, and without a flicker of emotion, cleaned them on the dead men's shirts and slid them back to their concealed sheaths, one in his boot, two in the strapping across his chest and shoulders. He grinned quietly to himself. His response in the face of a direct threat had been fast, his aim accurate. The blades, as ever, had served him well. But what of Darringo?

Had the bandido fallen deep into a cleft or creek? Was he injured and unconscious, or was he even now climbing stealthily back to the ledge, watchful of the hawk but equally determined to seek retribution for the killing of his men? That would be an instinctive reaction.

Or maybe the speed and accuracy of the blades had warned him off, at least temporarily. Maybe he would sneak back to wherever he had his mountain hideout and round up a fresh band who would wait then for the man to make the next move, lurking like lions in the rocks and crags.

He grunted, shielded his eyes against the fierce glare and scanned the surrounds. No sounds, nothing moving save the still circling hawk. The shadows stared but for the moment anyhow had no living eyes. He pulled at the brim of his hat and crossed back to the body of the murdered young man, squatted and examined the body in more detail. There was nothing that might hint at an identity, and it was doubtful if Darringo and his men had cared a deal who he was. He had simply been here, presumably alone, certainly armed but vulnerable and faced with hopeless odds once the *bandidos* had closed in for the kill.

Even so, Darringo had either discarded or dropped the chain necklet that lay in a crease between rocks.

The man turned it slowly through his fingers. Fine work using inexpensive silver. Probably of sentimental value, but nothing to indicate the identity of its owner. He flicked it into the palm of his hand and pocketed it.

Time to be moving, he decided. He would not go in search of Darringo. The *bandidos* would track him soon enough. He would cover the body of the young man, drag the sidekicks into the darker overhangs — the buzzards would soon be gathering — then mount up and put this sun-baked bandit country behind him before nightfall.

He had heard tell back East of a border town hereabouts name of Red Creeks. The sort of place, it was said, where a man might rest easy, no questions asked. That would do just fine.

The man was mounted up and riding within the hour, the hawk, long since joined by others, still circling soundlessly in its vigil over the dead.

★ ★ ★

Charlie Roy was certain, his mind made up: the grey smudge of dust cloud he had been watching from his veranda for the past hour was a lone rider heading this way. And at a fair lick of a pace judging by the distance he had covered since sun-up.

A stranger, that much could be safely wagered. None of the folk of Red Creeks used the mountain trail north. Too dangerous. Too many *bandidos* roaming the hills, scavenging, robbing, looting and murdering for whatever they saw as easy pickings. Specially if they were led by that scumbag Darringo, who attacked and pillaged at will and controlled the trails and tracks to both the north and west. Nobody tangled with Darringo and neither he nor his band of lawless sidekicks and gunslingers had ever been brought to book. These days nobody tried.

Charlie smacked his lips and creaked his rocker gently on the shadowed veranda. Maybe the approaching rider had crossed Darringo's path. Maybe he had gotten lucky and escaped. Sure as hell looked as if he was in some hurry to put the mountains behind him.

Or maybe he was just another fellow with a past heading for the border to avoid somebody with a vendetta or a lawman. Red Creeks had seen them all, and would again. The border town was the last stop for many before crossing into Mexico. For some it became permanent. They ended their days on Boot Hill.

No saying what Fate had in store for this one.

Charlie reached for his cherrywood pipe, tamped tobacco into the bowl and lit it thoughtfully, his gaze still flicking to the oncoming dust cloud. The fellow would be thirsty, dusty and worn through by the time he reached town. Same went for his mount. First call would be Frank Riley's livery, then O'Mara's bar where the stranger would relish a beer before ordering a plate of steak and cackle-berries and asking the price of a room.

Maybe he would get to a shave and dollar-bit bath at Pete's place, but that would depend — it always did — on whether a casual enquiry about the law hereabouts met with the stranger's approval. If it did, he would shave and clean up, maybe sleep some, take a woman. If not, he would ride. Last fellow through Red Creeks had cleared town within the hour on mention of Sheriff Grove's particular dislike of horse-thieves and rustlers.

So what might this fellow be riding from, pondered Charlie, behind a drifting spiral of pipe smoke?

It had to be something big — big enough and deep enough to force a man to flee his own territory for a face-less, nameless existence in a country where few questions were ever asked, and none at all if you had money. There life was cheap, if sometimes short-lived once across the border, and the living anonymous if that happened to be the way you wanted it.

So, mused Charlie, was it murder, rape, robbery, all three, that the fellow was riding from, or was he plain too far the wrong side of the law to find his way back? There was never any telling. Such fellows just rode in and you had no choice as to who or what they were. The good, the bad and the darndest of sonofabitch scumbags. It was like Charlie had always said: Red Creeks had seen them all. And here was just another in the long line.

Even so, he would be there at O'Mara's along with the rest to give the poor devil the once-over.

4

But he was not just another in the long line of arrivals at O'Mara's bar, and that was Charlie Roy's problem. And he was not alone in his surmising. Smoky O'Mara himself — so called because of the cigar clamped permanently between his gleaming teeth — was equally confused, as was Sheriff Grove. Frank Riley up at the livery had spotted it straight off, minute the fellow walked his weary mount to the stabling back of the forge.

'No doubtin' in my mind,' he confided to the group of town men gathered in the shade on the boardwalk fronting the saloon. 'Saw it in a flash — he ain't carryin' a weapon. Not a snitch. Not even wearin' a gunbelt,' he nodded knowingly. 'So what do yuh make of that? He ain't one of your reg'lar scumbags. Nothin' like.'

'Then who in tarnation is he?' an old man asked, rolling a twist of tobacco round his mouth. 'He give a name?'

'Not to me he ain't,' Frank had answered.

'Nor me,' the sheriff supported, easing to the batwings to catch a glimpse of the stranger seated at a table at the far end of the bar. 'Mebbe he'll get to talkin' to Smoky once his belly's packed.'

'Or mebbe,' Charlie offered, refilling his pipe, 'he's just a fellow travellin' through. No more, no less. There's gotta be some.'

'But not in Red Creeks!' Frank grinned. 'Not in my lifetime, anyhow. You name me one we've had through here these past years. You can't, 'cus Red Creeks ain't here for the likes of such men. We're here for scum on the run. Always have been, and this fella, when it comes to it, ain't goin' to be no different, gun or no gun.'

The old man rolled the chewing tobacco and spat carefully into the

24

dusty main street. 'Where's he from? Anybody got a hint?'

The sheriff shrugged his shoulders along with Frank.

'Out of the mountains — and that's about as much, damn near all, we know,' Charlie offered, curling a spiral of fresh smoke from his pipe. 'I watched him from the minute he first appeared. Soon after first light. A dust cloud no bigger than your thumbnail, but headin' fast, real fast, our way. Watched him 'til sun-up.' Charlie drew reflectively on his pipe. 'Didn't ease none 'til a mile out of town. Slowed then, like he was takin' in what he could see, but there weren't nothin' nervy about him. Didn't strike me as a fella lookin' out for trouble. Nossir, I reckoned for him bein' just one almighty slice thankful to have made it.' Charlie paused to watch the spiralling smoke. 'Can't say more or be fairer.'

The others gathered on the boardwalk nodded and grunted their understanding.

'Well, he sure weren't for bein' talkative when he hit my place,' Frank had said positively. 'Quiet as a roof mouse. Barely a word, save to ask my charges, settle his mount, check in his tack and ask if there was a sheriff in town and the way to the saloon. Paid in advance and left.' Frank eased closer to the men. 'But I'd seen that he weren't side-armed, and that struck me straight up as different, though it ain't to prove nothin'. Could be playin' it foxy.' He tapped a finger on the side of his nose. 'I seen fellas try that one before: standin' gun clean don't mean to say you ain't learned how to shoot.'

The others nodded again and stared in silence for a moment into the shadowy depths of the bar.

'Passed my place without a word,' the sheriff murmured. 'Lingered just long enough to fix I was there, then walked on, calm as a bird in a bush. I weren't for hailin' him — why should I? — so I just followed 'til he checked in here with Smoky.' He adjusted his hat and hitched his pants. 'Let's leave the fella to eat, then we'll get to talkin'.'

★   ★   ★

'Name's McKee. Just that.' The man volunteered his identity to Sheriff Grove, Charlie, Frank Riley, Smoky O'Mara and an audience of town men gathered in the saloon bar for their ritual evening's drinking an hour after sundown. 'And I ain't here for what I'm guessin' most of the visitors to Red Creeks have in mind: I'm not on the run and I ain't for crossin' the border,' he added, with a steady gaze over the watching faces.

'Well, that makes a refreshin' change!' a voice piped from the already smoke-hazed gloom.

'Glad to hear it,' said the sheriff, easing the sweaty tightness of his hat. 'But you sure hit town at some lick, accordin' to Charlie.'

'Don't dispute it,' agreed the man, leaning back in his chair at the bar-side table. 'Not surprisin', given that I was reckonin' on a certain Juan Darringo and his *bandidos* mebbe sittin' close on my butt.'

'We know Darringo well enough,' muttered Frank. 'Crossed him too many times.'

'If you'd been tanglin' with Darringo back there in the hills, you were lucky to get away,' said Grove. 'How did it happen?'

McKee told his story of finding the stripped body of the young man, of his encounter with Darringo, the subsequent events that led to the killings and his final ride from the rocks in a dry, matter-of-fact tone, sparing no details and none of the grim reality of his survival. His audience listened in silence, without interruption, without so much as the scrape of a boot or clink of a glass to disturb the flow.

'All that was left was this,' he concluded, laying the silver neck chain on the table. 'Not a deal, but somebody might recognize it.'

The sheriff and the town men pressed closer, each in his turn taking the chain in his fingers to examine it. A half-dozen bar girls had similarly passed it among themselves, but, like the men, finally pronounced that none of them had seen it before, certainly not being worn by anyone here in Red Creeks.

'Half figured that might be the case,' said McKee, pocketing the chain. 'It was a long shot, anyhow.'

'Worth a try,' puffed Smoky O'Mara from behind the swirling cloud of a freshly lit cigar. 'Point is, mister, you took out three of Darringo's men, and that, believe me, is mebbe the best news we've had hereabouts in months. You bet to it.'

'Not if the rat decides to ride in here with a bunch of his *bandidos* it ain't,' called an old man at a corner table.

'And you didn't shoot one of 'em . . . Just the knives,' murmured Frank as if to himself. 'Should've figured it minute I set eyes on you. Should've said — '

'So what now, Mr McKee?' clipped the sheriff, pouring himself another drink at the bar. 'You plannin' on stayin' in Red Creeks a while?'

'Day or so,' said McKee, coming to his feet. 'Rest up, take on some fresh supplies, then head west. No place special . . . '

Perhaps there had never been a 'special place' for the man, Charlie Roy had reflected quietly to himself in his rocker on the veranda some hours later. McKee had the look of being in search of somewhere to settle his roots. A man who had wandered and was still wandering, but who was no loose-handled drifter with a chip on his shoulder. Any man who could handle a knife as he apparently could and take out three of Darringo's fast-shooting *bandidos*, was nobody's fool. And Juan Darringo would know that, and not forget it, or bury his need for revenge. That would come soon enough.

Charlie lingered through two pipes and a generous measure of his home-made hooch, gazed long and hard and with a measure of some nostalgia at the sprawling mass of the distant hills and peaks before finally calling it a day.

He had known the hills for most of his life; scouted and travelled through and over them, and seen most of what they had to offer. The arrival out of them that day of the man called McKee was just another tale to add to memories.

Or so he thought then.

5

For Sheriff Grove the problem of McKee's arrival in Red Creeks was how soon he would leave. As he told Smoky O'Mara the following morning, 'I ain't for havin' a loose keg of dynamite on the premises any longer than absolutely necessary. If what he says is true and he has taken out three of Darringo's men single-handed — and I ain't for doubtin' the fella's word, you understand — but if that is the case, then believe me, Darringo ain't goin' to take it lyin' down. That's a fact. He'll hunt the man to the death if it's the last thing he does. That, too, is a fact, my friend.'

'You bet,' O'Mara agreed, nodding like a bird behind a cloud of cigar smoke. 'I wouldn't be standin' in his boots for nothin'. Add that to your facts.'

'So has he said any more about leavin'?'

'Not to me he ain't. Stays in his room for the most part. Don't mix none. Not much of a drinkin' man, and the girls don't seem to interest him over much. Keeps himself to himself.'

'Stay listenin',' Grove ordered. 'McKee mentions anythin' about pullin' out, I wanna be the first to know. Mebbe we'll get lucky and he'll leave before Darringo figures Red Creeks is where he's holed up.'

'Sure,' O'Mara agreed. 'I just get to wonderin' what a fella like him does for a livin'. Don't seem to be down on his luck. Pays in advance, no question. So where does the money come from?'

'Just don't ask,' the sheriff urged. 'We might not like the answer . . . '

A group of town men — Charlie Roy, Frank Riley, Doc Whipple and storekeeper Aaron Brewin predominant among a crowd of others — would gather regularly through the hot afternoons and sultry evenings to mull over once again McKee's incredible story and, more importantly, the prospect of

Darringo's retaliation and when and how it might come.

'Anytime, anywhere, if you're askin' me,' Frank pronounced. 'Out there in the hills, or down here, right in town, mebbe in this very street. All depends when the mood hits the rat and the blood's boilin' fierce enough.'

That was Doc Whipple's opinion. 'I figure for Darringo not riskin' a shoot-out here in town. There's too much at stake for the sake of the killin' of one man.' His view had met with a murmur of approval from the others. 'No, I figure for him waitin' til McKee moves out, mebbe back to the hills or wherever he chooses. Darringo operates best when he's on his own ground. So I say he'll bide his time and keep watchin'.'

Aaron Brewin, a fiercely forthright and proud town man who aspired, should the chance ever arise, to some recognized civic role, took a more deliberate view. 'I say why wait on either man? Why don't we put our situation direct to McKee? Tell him straight up how we feel; how we reckon for the town bein' at some risk. Damn it, why don't we tell him to leave? He's hardly in any position to refuse us, is he?'

'You mean turn him out for Darringo's pack to hunt down at will?' an old man said.

'Not just like that,' Brewin flustered. 'Mebbe we could ride with him so far, 'til we figured for him bein' safe?'

'How far's far?' the man persisted. 'How safe is safe?'

'Heck, how should I know? All I'm sayin' is — '

Charlie Roy interrupted with a carefully timed cough. 'Mebbe the fella ain't for leavin'. You thought of that?'

'You mean he's figurin' to stay in Red Creeks?' Frank asked.

'Could be. Don't see a whole lot stoppin' him. Free country, ain't it? Ain't nothin' to say he couldn't settle right here in town, not if he's a mind to.'

'And you reckon he has?'

'Well, now, that is somethin' we can ask him,' Charlie suggested.

But the question was never put. The answer came soon after sun-up the next day.

* * *

They thundered into town from the north. Twelve strong on sweat-lathered mounts. Hard-riding, weathered men, more used to the plains' winds, hill rains and mountain winters than the soft comforts of town.

Their leader introduced himself to Sheriff Grove as Edgar Rosen 'land-owner, rancher, cattleman; ten thousand acres and fast growing out Montana way.'

'You're a long ways from home, Mr Rosen,' the sheriff had observed politely but pointedly.

'And with good reason,' Rosen growled as if about to issue a string of commands. 'I'm lookin' for a man, a very special man — my son as it happens — last heard of headin' south out of Michaelstown. Me and my boys have travelled this far without a sound or sight of him, and you don't get much further south than Red Creeks. Close to the border, ain't you? So what I'm here to ask is: has anybody seen anythin' of my son?' He produced a bent, battered, sepia-tinted photograph from inside his shirt and handed it to the sheriff. 'There's a thousand dollar reward for any man who can make a positive identification. Circulate it. Meantime, me and the boys will look to our mounts, wash and clean up. Point us in the right direction, if you'll be so obligin'.'

Rosen's arrival in town, the news of his quest and his generally commanding manner quickly made their mark. There was a constant stream of folk to the boardwalk fronting Sheriff Grove's office where the photograph of Rosen's son and the announcement of the thousand-dollar reward had been pinned to the notice board.

'Sure could use that sorta money,' one man had remarked ruefully, scratching his bald head, 'but, hell, I never set eyes on the fella. I'd wager for him never havin' set a foot in Red Creeks.'

'And I'd second that,' agreed livery owner, Frank Riley. 'Ain't nobody rides into this town without my knowin' to him. What you say, Charlie, that young fella ain't never been here, has he?'

'I'd reckon not,' Charlie nodded. 'But if he was headin' out of Michaelstown like Rosen says he was, then he had only one trail to follow: due south straight as an arrow. Question is — why had he left Montana for Michaelstown, and was he alone when he pulled out?'

'We ain't never goin' to know the answer to that,' Doc Whipple suggested. 'It mebbe ain't our business, anyhow.'

'Tell you somethin',' an old wag grinned, shielding his voice, 'if I had a pa like Rosen I'd be for ridin' south! Hell, fella's got a mouth on him like he was spittin' peppers!'

Sheriff Grove had given until early

evening before heading for O'Mara's saloon where Rosen and his men had chosen to rest up and relax.

'Sorry, Mr Rosen,' he explained, 'looks like you're goin' to draw a blank as far as your son bein' seen in Red Creeks is concerned. Don't seem he's headed this way at all, which means — '

'I know what that *probably* means, Sheriff,' Rosen snapped. 'It means he may have crossed the border somewhere hereabouts and is now in Mexico.' He thudded a fist on the table in front of him. 'But I reckon not. In fact, I *say* not.'

'Mebbe we should get to scourin' around a deal closer,' the tallest and stockiest of Rosen's men offered, pouring himself a hefty measure of whiskey from a half-empty bottle. 'Could be young Johnny got kinda diverted or somethin'. Lost in them hills and mountains we skirted round. No sayin' to what can happen on a long trail.'

'If he was travellin' alone — ' began Grove.

Rosen thudded the table again. 'We don't know that,' he growled. 'We don't know nothin' of what's happened. Nobody does.'

It was at that moment that the bat-wings to the bar creaked open and McKee, the sepia photograph in his right hand, stepped into the soft glow of the lantern light.

'But I know what happened,' he said quietly.

6

Charlie Roy closed his eyes on the dark moonlit night and rocked gently to the turmoil of his thoughts. This was no time for sleep. No time for anything save to figure quietly the implications of what had happened since the creaking open of the bat-wings at O'Mara's bar, and how it was that he, a long since retired old hill scout, had gotten himself so involved in the events that had followed . . .

Edgar Rosen and his men heard McKee out without interruption and barely a movement, their eyes fixed and focused on his face as if watching his story enacted before them.

'This was the man I found, leastways one very like him. The body was in some state,' he said, placing the photograph on the table. 'Your son, I'm told. I'm sorry.'

Rosen had continued to stare into McKee's face, his breathing heavy, his expression suddenly gaunt and drained. Sheriff Grove shifted uncomfortably, conscious of the saloon beginning to fill with a shuffling mob of town men, curious bar girls and O'Mara's thickening cloud of cigar smoke.

It was a full minute before the stocky, whiskey-swigging sidekick eased to the bar to lay his hand on a fresh bottle and address McKee through an unblinking stare. 'Hold on there, fella,' he grunted, a gathering slur deepening his voice. 'We're goin' to need a whole sight more evidence before acceptin' your word on this.'

A slimmer, shifty-eyed sidekick agreed. 'Anybody could spin out a yarn such as you've just told. Sure they could, specially when there's a thousand dollars hangin' on it.'

'I don't rate Mr McKee for bein' no yarn-spinner,' clipped Sheriff Grove, stiffening his shoulders.

'And that goes for the rest of us,'

Aaron Brewin added. 'We've all heard McKee's story. The man ain't no liar. No good reason to be, has he?' The town men murmured their approval.

'That's straight up, Mr Rosen,' beamed O'Mara, wafting aside the smoke. 'I get 'em all through here, every measure and mood of man you can imagine, and I'd vouch for McKee any day. You got my word on it.' More smoke drifted to the rafters. 'Anyhow, you don't need my word or anyone else's come to that. McKee's got the neck chain. Show 'em, fella, let 'em see what you found out there.'

The tense silence that followed seemed to descend like a curtain. The stocky sidekick's hand slid from the whiskey bottle. His leaner partner frowned. A bright beading of sweat broke across Rosen's brow. Sheriff Grove stiffened again. O'Mara's cigar smoke thickened. The bar girls and town men waited, their eyes riveted on McKee's face.

'Neck chain?' Rosen had hissed at

last. 'You found a neck chain?'

'Picked it from the rocks close to where I found the body.' McKee spoke quietly, firmly as he slid the silver chain to the table.

Rosen stared at it without a sound, his fingers dead at his side.

'I figure for the *bandidos* either droppin' it, or ratin' it of no value,' McKee had added.

'That was my son's,' muttered Rosen at last. 'That was Johnny's . . . '

★   ★   ★

There was never any doubt in Rosen's mind. The silver chain found in the rocks by McKee had belonged to his son, Johnny. He had been given it on his seventeenth birthday. But there were also some long, painful minutes of a silence broken only by the tick of the saloon bar clock before Rosen finally dared to finger the chain, clear his thoughts and his throat to speak again.

'I want the sonofabitch who killed my

son brought to book,' he croaked. 'You hear that? You hear what I'm sayin'?' His glare was fierce and defiant. 'I want him dead. As dead as they get. And I want them henchmen of his dead alongside him. Is that clear?'

'You got it, boss,' said one of his men to the murmured agreement of the others. 'Just as soon as we can get to it.'

'Now hold on there,' Sheriff Grove counselled, with a sudden sweep of his arm. 'That's easy enough to say, Mr Rosen, and I sympathize real deep with how you must be feelin' — hell, you got good cause for your anger, but trackin' down Juan Darringo and his bunch, let alone bringin' them to justice, ain't so simple as it sounds. And frankly I doubt — '

'What will it take?' Rosen snapped. 'Name it. Money ain't no object.'

'And money ain't the answer neither.'

Rosen rounded on McKee, the glare still lit as if on fire. 'You've earned your reward, mister. The thousand dollars is yours, but I'll double it, treble it if you say so, for you to lead me and my men into them mountains to where you found Johnny and then help me find this Darringo scum. What do you say?'

McKee simply stared, his gaze not shifting an inch from Rosen's face.

'You're goin' to need more than McKee for what you got in mind,' Grove grunted. 'A whole sight more.'

'That's true enough, Mr Rosen,' Smoky O'Mara nodded through another cloud of smoke. 'There ain't no fella walkin' this earth as can tackle them mountains without knowin' them like the back of his hand, specially where Darringo's concerned. Ain't that so, Doc?'

'I'd reckon,' Doc Whipple agreed. 'To Darringo the mountains are home. He's lived best part of his life among them, knows them like old friends — and used them as his deadliest weapon. It don't matter how many men you get to ride with you, Mr Rosen, Darringo will use the mountains against you, turn them on you like a pack of hungry wolves. Only way you could get even a half chance of succeedin' is to have a mountain scout along of you, and the only decent one of that breed hereabouts is retired. Tell him, Charlie, before our friend here gets to cajolin' you out of that rocker of yours . . . '

★ ★ ★

Charlie Roy opened his eyes with a start, brought the rocker to a sudden halt and stared deep into the night.

He could make out the line of the mountains from his veranda even at this hour: Eagle point to the right, Snake Pass and the Long Ridge to the left, with just the faintest suggestion of Cloud Peak and the notorious Rock Tor almost dead ahead.

He knew them all, had lived with them, fought among them and, like Darringo and his men, used them as his weapons, but that had been long ago when Red Creeks had been little more than a huddle of shacks and a handful of folk under canvas.

And now here he was letting himself be talked into some hare-brained scheme to trek into them again with a Montana land baron drunk on his hatred of Darringo and now seeking no less than brutal revenge for the death of his only son, and a stranger, name of McKee, who was for certain top of the *bandidos'* list of most wanted men.

He must be mad.

7

'I gotta say this, Charlie Roy — you're plumb crazy and that's no foolin'!' Sheriff Grove strode the length of the veranda, turned sharply on his heel and stared like a hunting hawk through the early morning light at Charlie still settled in his rocker. 'And you know somethin',' he went on, 'now that you've had time to sleep on it, I think you know you're plumb crazy.'

'I ain't slept on it,' mumbled Charlie. 'In fact, I ain't slept.'

'Not surprised. What on earth's gotten into you, Charlie? Why'd you go agreein' to ride with Rosen and his men? Hell, you ain't that desperate for money, but you're sure a sight the wrong side of fifty to be draggin' your butt through them hills and mountains. Would've figured for you havin' had a bellyful of that. And then there's

Darringo. Now just what — '

'I ain't for lettin' McKee go back there without somebody who knows the mountains at his side. He'll just get himself killed if he goes in cold again, and that don't seem neither right nor fair.'

The sheriff pushed his hat clear of his brow and scratched his head. 'Well, that's mighty considerate of you, Charlie Roy,' he mocked. 'Sure it is, seein' as how you hardly know the fella and he sounds a whole lot more likely to be able to take care of himself than you are. Plus the fact he's goin' to be surrounded by Rosen's guns, and plus the fact he's bein' paid a heap of dollars to risk his life. He'll know the odds. He's doin' the gamblin'. You're just bein' plain crazy!'

'So you've said,' murmured Charlie, setting the rocker into motion again, 'but that don't change nothin'. I've given my word to McKee and I'll stand by it.'

Grove sighed and settled his hat.

'Well, I've had my say. Nothin' more I can do save to wish you good luck and — though it goes a mite against my judgement — promise I'll be lookin' to you somehow or other. Right now I couldn't raise so much as the town drunk to ride along of me to the mountains, but there'd be a willin' enough posse for you, Charlie. If we haven't heard from you or of you in five days, the town men will hit the trail. You've got my word on it.'

'Won't be necessary,' muttered Charlie, 'I'll be back just as soon as we're all through.'

'You're a stubborn man, Charlie Roy, and you've sure got a way of lookin' to your pride. McKee and Rosen are lucky to have you ridin' with 'em.' The sheriff walked slowly back to the steps at the far end of the veranda. 'I hear Rosen's plannin' to pull out at noon. His men are puttin' stores and pack horses together now. You'd best — '

But that was as far as Grove got. In the next moment a gangly-limbed, spotty-faced youth had rounded the side of the clapboard house in a state of high excitement and near to bursting lungs.

'You gotta come quick, Sheriff,' the youth spluttered. 'There's been a killin'!'

'A what?' shouted Grove.

The youth gulped and thumped his chest. 'Like I said, Sheriff, a killin'. McKee's knifed one of that Rosen bunch.'

* * *

And so he had. Right there at the back of O'Mara's saloon bar. The dead man, as the throng of town folk gathered at the bat-wings were quick to inform the sheriff, was the shifty-eyed sidekick among Rosen's men who had first hinted that McKee might be a yarn spinner out to grab a fast dollar.

Doc Whipple was examining the body as Grove came to his side.

'What happened here?' he asked,

adjusting the set of his hat. 'Anybody see anythin'?'

'Blade straight into the neck,' said Doc. 'And delivered with some force and speed. Fella would've died instantly.' He came upright from his squatting position. One of the bar girls says she saw what happened. She was here fixing herself a hangover cure.'

The sheriff grunted and stared closer at the body, 'Fella's clutchin' a Colt. He draw on McKee?'

'That's what the girl says.'

'Where's McKee now? And where's Rosen f'chris'sake? This is one of his men.'

'McKee, Rosen and the girl, name of Blanche — she's new — are all with O'Mara in his back room waitin' on you.'

Grove grunted again. 'You got any opinions on this, Doc?'

'Difficult to disagree with what the girl's told me. Tell you somethin', though, McKee weren't foolin' none or boastin' when he told how he took out

Darringo's men. You bet he wasn't. I ain't never seen a knife killin' like this before. Never.'

★ ★ ★

McKee stood with his back to the window, a relaxed, easy look on his otherwise expressionless face. Rosen was at his side, his arms folded, stare unblinking and fixed but already darkening with impatience.

The bar girl had seated herself in a chair at the baize-covered table, where she twitched, sniffed and twisted a wet handkerchief through her fingers. O'Mara seemed to be cast in stone, an unlit cigar in one hand, a vast bandanna hanging in the other, his face a mass of sweating bewilderment.

'Let's get this over with fast,' growled Rosen on a heave of chafing breath. 'I want to be clear of town by noon.'

Grove eyed the rancher sharply. 'All in good time, Mr Rosen. *My* time,' he said pointedly, turning then to McKee.

'Care to tell me what happened, mister?'

'Self-defence,' blurted Rosen. 'Plain as the nose on your face.'

'I'll be the judge of that,' snapped the sheriff.

'Blanche here reckons — ' began O'Mara, laying an arm across the girl's shoulders.

The girl sniffed and dabbed at a new stream of tears.

'All right, all right,' urged Grove. 'We aint gettin' nowhere this way. Let's hear McKee.'

The man took a step away from the bright morning light at the window. 'Simple enough, Sheriff,' he said calmly, his gaze still relaxed. 'Fella out there — name of Lester Cook, one of Mr Rosen's men — came to me while I was havin' an early coffee in the bar and suggested again that my story of findin' the body of Johnny Rosen could easily be a whole heap of lies. I reminded him of the neck chain I'd recovered, but before I could go any further he'd drawn his holstered Colt and from where I was standin' was pretty obviously set to use it.'

'That's right, Mr Grove,' sniffed the girl. 'I saw it all. I was right there in the bar fixin' . . . well, never mind. But I saw what happened, you bet, and that fella was sure as jack-rabbits goin' to use that piece.'

'Then what happened?' said the Sheriff. 'You drew a blade, McKee?'

'He did that, you bet,' blurted the girl, brushing at the stain of tears, her bloodshot eyes flashing. 'Did he! Faster than you can say it, Mr Grove, just like a sudden light. Know what I mean? One minute that scumbag was standin' there, gun in his hand, hellfire in his eyes, and the next he was dead, just like that, a knife in his neck. Then only silence. McKee removed the blade, cleaned it and we sent young Tommy runnin' for you.' She shuddered, sniffed, tossed her loose hair into her neck, and sat back in the chair under O'Mara's comforting arm. 'That was the size of it, Mr Grove. That was self-defence if ever I saw it.'

'Just as I said,' blustered Rosen, crossing the room to the door. 'Fella was never one of my best. He's no loss to me or anybody else. McKee has done us all a favour. Bury the rat. I'll leave you the money.' He stiffened his shoulders. 'Now can we please get on with our preparations for pullin' out? We're wastin' valuable time here.'

'You satisfied, Sheriff?' asked O'Mara. 'I can vouch for Blanche's word here. She may be fresh in town, but she ain't no liar, I'll wager to that.'

Grove's attention focused on McKee. 'Seems straightforward enough. That was self-defence the way I've heard it.'

'From an eye-witness,' said O'Mara, suddenly conscious of the unlit cigar in his fingers.

'You still goin' along with this mountain trek?' asked Grove, his gaze tightening on McKee. 'Seems to me you might have some resentment among the company you'll be keepin'.'

'Nonsense,' flashed Rosen. 'Lester Cook was a bad apple. Should've spotted it months back. My men are under my control. Don't nobody forget it. McKee rides with me, as does that scout fella, Charlie Roy.'

'Charlie Roy is way past mountain trekkin',' retorted Grove. 'Told him as much this mornin', but he ain't for listenin'. Plain crazy in my book.'

'He's his own man, Sheriff,' said Rosen. 'As is McKee here. Fella has his options, makes his choices, and you can't say fairer. Now, shall we get on?'

* * *

Doc Whipple relaxed in the chair on the veranda outside O'Mara's saloon and squinted at the activity in the sunlit street. 'I'm sorely tempted to call this a bad day in Red Creeks,' he murmured within earshot of Aaron Brewin, Frank Riley, Smoky O'Mara and Sheriff Grove. 'In fact, I will say it, this *is* a bad day in Red Creeks.'

'No good will come of it for Charlie,' added the livery owner. 'He ain't up to it.'

Aaron Brewin sighed deeply as he watched Rosen marshalling his men and the trailed pack-horses under the watchful eyes of McKee and Charlie. 'Pride,' he said as if to himself. 'It's all down to pride. Charlie reckons for bein' able to ride them hills and mountains just like he did twenty years ago. And when it came to scoutin' there weren't none better. But, heck, that was way back. Charlie ain't the man he was. Don't he realize that?'

'No tellin' him,' said the sheriff. 'He just ain't for listenin'.'

'Well, I'll tell you fellas somethin' for nothin': McKee ain't nobody's fool,' nodded Smoky O'Mara, lighting a fresh cigar with a flourish. 'There's a fact for you if you like. Way he handled that knife back there, accordin' to Blanche, was a sight to behold. If there's anybody can take care of himself against Darringo, it's McKee. Yessir, I'd wager on that for a certainty.'

'T'ain't Darringo and his men that bothers me,' murmured Doc again. 'It's Rosen out there and his bunch.'

'You referrin' to the killin' earlier on?' asked the storekeeper.

'Precisely that,' said Doc. 'Why did the fella bait McKee like he says he did? What was the point? Rosen was already set on ridin' with the fella.'

'Rosen couldn't give a damn,' clipped the sheriff. 'He's as cold as a fish.'

The men were silent for some minutes before Doc said quietly, 'Why was Johnny Rosen alone out there in the mountains?'

But nobody answered as the call went up in the bustling street for the riders to make column and move out.

Charlie Roy did not look back.

8

Charlie rode easy through the first miles out of Red Creeks across the sweeping emptiness of the plains to the distant foothills.

He had been ordered at the outset to take up point at the head of the column alongside McKee. 'If you're scoutin' for this outfit, Mr Roy, and I'm payin',' Rosen had growled, 'then that's exactly what you'll do. You hear that, men? Mr Roy is the boss when it comes to the trail and ain't answerable to nobody save me. He'll work directly with Mr McKee. No interference, no messin'. Let that be understood.'

McKee rode in silence, his body relaxed to the steady pace of his mount, his gaze on the far horizon always busy and probing. But his thoughts, mused Charlie, might have been anywhere, though he doubted if he was the sort of fellow who would dwell greatly on the killing of men who had threatened him. That he would have seen as being necessary to survival. As to why he had agreed to lead Rosen to where he had buried the body of his son, that needed no figuring. It was all a matter of money. No more, no less.

As to whether or not he would tangle with Darringo again, that was another question. Who could say? It would depend on a whole heap of events — and Charlie Roy was not for guessing. He had his own thoughts to settle.

Fact was, Sheriff Grove was maybe dead-eyed right: he was acting plain crazy. But, heck, the open plains right here beneath him, the clean-edged winds, high, clear skies and the prospect of the mountains, were a sight more satisfying right now than a rocker and a shady veranda. You bet!

He tightened the reins and eased the mount back a stride to join McKee. 'By my reckonin', your encounter with Darringo and his boys took place on the lower reaches of Long Ridge,' he called across the jangle of tack and creak of leather. 'Your description fits. Happens to be one of the *bandidos*' favourite stalkin' grounds. Main trail from the north narrows there before creepin' round Cloud Peak. Anyhow, that's where we're headin'. Foothills by nightfall. We'll rest up and ride for Eagle Point at first light and make Snake Pass and the Ridge by noon — if we stay lucky.'

McKee nodded. 'Thanks,' he answered.

'No need for thanks, mister. Only doin' the job I signed up for.'

'I meant thanks for agreein' to ride.'

Charlie grunted. 'Just hope you figure on makin' enough for that trip west you were plannin'.'

'We'll give it a good shot, Mr Roy. But why are you out here? Don't tell me it's the money.'

'No, Mr McKee, this is my country. My hills, my mountains. I'm just back among old friends, and glad to be so.'

'In spite of Darringo and the

bandidos?' said McKee, his gaze tight on the horizon of foothills and high, snow-tipped peaks. 'They don't worry you none?'

'Oh, they worry me, Mr McKee. It'd be a fool man who didn't worry when Darringo's skulkin' around these hills and rocks. Never no sayin' to what he might do, or when.'

'You figure he's already seen us?'

Charlie flicked the reins through his fingers. 'You can stake your life on it. He's got look-outs watchin' pretty well round the clock of daylight hours. He'll be watchin', waitin', reckonin'.' He glanced quickly at McKee. 'And notin' that you're among the riders.' Charlie flicked the reins again and clicked his tongue for the mount to move ahead. 'But meantime, let's make it to the foothills, eh?'

★　★　★

'Well, Mr Roy, how are our chances shapin' up? And no hidin' the facts, if

64

you please. I ain't for fancy talk.' Edgar Rosen stood with his back to the scrub and branch fire, legs apart, hands on hips, his face a glistening mass of concentration. The stocky, shifty-eyed sidekick he had since introduced as Raps Malone, stood at his side, a whiskey bottle in one hand, a tin mug in the other. The others lounged and relaxed at the edge of the glow. McKee as ever was alone in the shadows that reached like black limbs and muscles from the scatterings of pines and rocks.

Charlie turned from the line-hitched mounts and strolled slowly back to the firelight. 'A mite too early to say, I'd reckon,' he said, tamping a filling of tobacco into his cherrywood pipe. 'We've made good time. Cleared the plain easy enough. We'll ride for Eagle Point at sun-up.'

'And Darringo?' asked Malone. 'What about him?'

'Nothin' about him,' said Charlie bluntly. 'He's here, somewhere, and he knows we're here. But he won't be for makin' a move yet.'

'Too many of us,' sneered Malone, pouring whiskey into the tin mug.

'Numbers don't threaten Darringo. He's got the mountains.'

'And just what do you mean by that?' The man gulped at the drink.

'Darringo uses every one of these rocks, every creek, ridge, ledge, track, like they were a part of an army. Don't be fooled, mister, in the right hands with the right know-how they can be a powerful force.'

'Well, I'm all for trustin' to guns, old-timer, and we've got plenty of them,' sneered Malone again. 'Ain't that so, Mr Rosen?'

'I don't want no gun-happy blazin' neither,' snapped Rosen. 'I want to see Johnny buried decent and I want Darringo dead — in that order.' His face gleamed in a surge of sweat. 'Only then do we hit the trail for Montana. Not until.'

'Yeah, well, you ain't goin' to get to Darringo save on his terms, when he's good and ready,' said Charlie lighting his pipe. 'And on ground of his choosin', make no mistake to that.'

'Darringo don't trouble me none,' mocked Malone, gazing round. 'The boys and me have taken out worse scum.' He gulped another mouthful of whiskey. 'McKee there should've finished the rat when he had the chance. Guess we'll have to do the job for him, eh, boys?'

The men murmured their agreement. McKee stayed silent; simply watchful. Charlie blew a long spiral of smoke.

Rosen stared into the night as if expecting Darringo to materialize in the moonlight. 'Go easy on that liquor, Malone,' was all he said, before nodding to Charlie and walking away to the shadows. 'Let's get some sleep,' he ordered.

But sleep was not so easy for Charlie. Now that he was out here, with Red Creeks, the familiar town faces, the settled order of his clapboard home, the day-to-day routine behind him, the questions and uncertainties were beginning to resurface.

Who was McKee? He still knew nothing about this man who handled a knife as if born with it, who showed nothing of his emotions in the killing of a man? Did anybody know him?

And what of Rosen? How far would his obsessive search for the remains of his son and seething revenge for his murder finally take him? More to the point, how far were others prepared to go in seeing that obsession pacified?

And then there was the swaggering, loose-lipped arrogance of Malone. He spelled trouble. Much more of that cheap tonsil varnish he had somehow managed to smuggle with him and the fists, if not the lead, would be flying.

Darringo was maybe twice the problem. He was the real uncertainty, the shadow that could come and go at will through these mountains without ever being seen, never heard, but never far away. Sometimes as close as a breath. Maybe Rosen had not yet got to figuring that. Malone certainly had not. But had McKee?

He was sleeping quiet now along with the others, save for the two posted guard, one at the hitch-line, a second watching the hills. But with McKee you might never know. Maybe, like Charlie right now and the posted guard, he too was watching.

You could bet your sweet life somebody was watching them.

* * *

It was an hour after sun-up on the following day that territorial Marshal Jim Keetch rode into Red Creeks on the little used trail from the East.

His first call was at the office of Sheriff Grove where, in Keetch's characteristic no-messing, no-frills bluntness he wanted to know if a fellow by the name of Johnny Rosen had been seen or heard of hereabouts. Rosen, he explained, was carrying a price of more than $5,000 on his head, wanted dead or alive, for the killing of homesteader Angus Scott and his wife, Emma, out Pinecuts way.

Grove invited the marshal to take a seat, share a pot of early-morning coffee while he told of what had been happening in Red Creeks these past days.

He figured he would find it interesting.

9

They went from the remains of the overnight camp-fire at the first hint of light. For Rosen and his men, the harsh scrub and rock track selected by Charlie for the trek to Eagle Point was tough going from the start.

'Stay quiet, in single file, and keep movin',' Charlie had insisted. 'This ain't no picnic and we ain't sight-seein'. Hold your mounts steady, no strayin', but we don't want no panic. Sounds hereabouts echo like ghosts wailin'.'

'What about Darringo?' Malone had been quick to ask through his bleary gaze.

'He'll be around, don't you fret. But he won't be for doin' nothin' yet. He'll prefer to let us get deeper before he shows himself.'

'And when do you figure that for bein'?' Rosen had clipped curtly, his

71

gaze already narrowed on the snow-line of the higher peaks.

Charlie had finished his pipe before answering. 'After Eagle Point would be my guess. But nothin's ever a certainty where Darringo is concerned. He roams these mountains like a wild cat — which is maybe just what he is.'

McKee rode close on Charlie's heels for the first hour, his concentration as fixed as ever on the lie of the land, the offshoot animal tracks, the sounds, shapes and soon the gathering strength of the sun and the stifling heat it brought with it.

'There's a freshwater pool at the Point,' Charlie had said, mopping at a beading of sweat. 'We'll rest up there; twenty minutes, no more. Then we make for Snake Pass. I'll be needin' your eyes and callin' on your memory once we sight the Ridge. Do you reckon you can find the body again?'

'I'll find it,' assured McKee.

'Meantime get back among the men and tell them to go easy on their canteens. At this height in this heat it pays to stay cautious. Don't take nothin' for granted . . . '

★ ★ ★

'You sure about this? I mean there can't be any mistake, can there? Situations like that and, well, a fella can get carried away. Easy enough. I've seen it before.' Doc Whipple swallowed and ran a finger round his sweat-sticky collar. 'You are sure?' he added quietly.

Marshal Keetch relaxed his arms on the table where he sat in the corner of O'Mara's saloon, and drummed his fingers quietly on the surface. He waited some moments, then settled his hands and spoke with the same certainty and authority he had shown some three hours back in Sheriff Grove's office.

'No doubt about it in my mind,' he began. 'Wouldn't be here otherwise. We have a reliable eyewitness whose word I wouldn't question.'

'And he actually saw what happened at the Scott homestead?' asked Aaron Brewin, lighting a thin cheroot. 'He was there?'

'Sure was. Fella had worked as a part-time hand for Scott these past twelve months. That day he had arrived early anxious to get to repairing a stretch of damaged fence. He saw three men ride in from the east. Figured they might be friends of Scott, so went back to his work. Thirty minutes later, Scott had been shot and his wife gagged, raped and killed. The three were riding clear, heading for the mountains within minutes.'

The marshal paused, slid his arms from the table and leaned back in his chair.

'Same fella rode hell-for-leather, raised me and recognized Rosen instantly from the Wanted poster I'd just nailed up at my office. Rosen, it seems, was already wanted out Clarion way for a similar shooting and rape.'

'So how long has the young rat been

terrorizin' the territory?' frowned Doc Whipple. 'And who are the scum he's ridin' with, and why, in God's name?'

'His pa must have known, surely?' added Frank Riley, pushing his hat to the back of his head. 'That must have been why he was chasing after the sonofabitch.'

O'Mara lit a cigar, blew smoke, and announced, 'I just don't figure it, and that's the truth.'

'Edgar Rosen was bein' a mite skimpy with the facts in the version of the story he fed yourselves and the fella you know as McKee,' said Keetch. 'My reckonin' would be that he knew full well why his son left the ranch in Montana, and very probably the side-kicks ridin' with him. Mebbe he got to hear of Johnny's exploits. Mebbe he could guess what he would get into. Mebbe he'd done it before. Whatever, he was in no two minds about givin' chase.'

'And now?' asked the sheriff. 'What do we do from here on? McKee ain't heard the truth, nor has Charlie. Where does that leave them? But if Darringo's killed Johnny — '

'And if Charlie and McKee are riskin' their lives for the body of a no-good sonofabitch who deserved to die anyhow — ' added Brewin.

Frank Riley thudded his fist on the bar. 'Hell, we should get out there right now. This very day. Organize a town posse. Charlie and McKee have got to know what's really gone on. Rosen ain't goin' to tell 'em, that's for sure. What do you reckon, Sheriff?'

'I say we saddle up and hit the trail by noon,' called an old-timer from the back of the bar. 'And I'm volunteerin' to ride with you. Charlie Roy don't deserve a fate like what's facin' him. Nossir, he don't. Darn fool should have stayed in that rocker.'

'T'ain't no good frettin' round what might have been,' piped a younger man. 'We gotta plan on what we do now. You got an opinion, Mr Keetch?'

The marshal came to his feet, crossed

the smoky bar to the bat-wings, and stared into the silent, sunlit street. He was a while before he spoke again. 'Personally speakin', I've got two choices: one, I can take the words of McKee and Edgar Rosen at face value and believe that Johnny Rosen died at the hands of Darringo and his men. The silver chain and Rosen's positive identification of it should be enough for me to say that some form of justice has been done. Ain't much of a comfort where the kin of the Scotts are concerned, but mebbe that's life.'

He paused a moment and turned to face the saloon-bar gathering. 'Or, two, I can ride out there into the mountains and go see for myself. And, more important, mebbe I can hear from Edgar Rosen just why, when and how this whole sorry mess began, and not least lend a hand to McKee and Charlie Roy.'

'And have you made a choice?' asked Doc Whipple.

'Yes,' said the marshal, 'I think I have . . . '

At about the same time that Marshal Keetch was addressing the town folk of Red Creeks in Smoky O'Mara's saloon bar, the hairs in Charlie Roy's neck were beginning to prickle. And it was not because of the heat.

For the first time that morning he was worried.

The line of riders had made steady progress along the track to Eagle Point in spite of the thickening heat, the difficulties of the terrain and, for all their hard talk, the men's general mood of unease and the unknown.

McKee had continued to be Charlie's second pair of eyes — keen, concentrated and focused, but even he had missed the shifting shadows on the higher reaches. He had not seen the sudden movement among boulders that might so easily have been mistaken for a scud of cloud — save that there were no clouds.

Nor, it seemed, had he spotted the

drifting into place of shapes where previously there had been simply a clutter of rocks. Four bulges had suddenly become five; two had moved slightly to the left, another to the right. But there were no sounds, no noticeable movements. The place might have been a deserted wilderness.

But it was far from that.

Charlie reckoned there were at least a dozen men watching from the slopes and ridges, and probably Darringo himself from somewhere in the deeper shade. With every yard the line progressed, Darringo's smile would broaden, his eyes narrow, his mind tick like a wound clock in its calculation of just how far he would let the riders go. Maybe into the tighter trail of Snake Pass, or the wilder sweep of the Long Ridge. Wherever, whenever he chose. The land was his . . .

'How far to your water pool, Mr Roy?' croaked Rosen on an obviously parched, dry throat.

'Comin' up,' answered Charlie, pointing ahead. 'Round the overhang there. Five minutes.'

The voices echoed, the clip of hoofs on rocks had thinned to the sound of cracking that spiralled through the air. A lone hawk, high against the backdrop of the cloudless blue, drifted silently into view.

Charlie swallowed and blinked on a surge of sweat as he urged his mount ahead of the column to round the overhang.

'Hell's teeth!' he cursed, through a grating hiss and stared in disbelief at the pool where a dead horse lay putrefying in the shallows. 'Darringo!' he hissed again.

It was then that three shots rang out and three men in the line behind him fell to the ground.

10

Horses snorted, hoofs crashed and clattered on rock. Men's voices rose in shouts and curses. 'Get into cover!' bellowed Rosen above the mayhem. More shots spat and blazed from the higher reaches of Eagle Point. Two riders fell from their mounts.

McKee rounded on the line and drove the men towards the shadowed cover of boulders to his left. 'This way!' he yelled. 'Scatter the horses.'

Charlie had already turned from the pool, slid from the saddle, urged his horse into cover and stumbled, a sweat-soaked mass, into the nearest sprawl of rocks. He blinked, gathered his breath and risked a glance back towards the track.

Five men lay dead in the shimmer of the searing sunlight. 'Sonofabitch,' he murmured to himself, at the same time narrowing his gaze instinctively on the higher rocks. No sign now of shapes; no hint of the glint of a barrel; no sounds. But Darringo had them pinned down sure enough, at the whim now of whatever he ordered.

Charlie switched his gaze to the track again as he sought to make out McKee and Rosen. Nothing of McKee at a first glance, but Rosen was clear, the upper half of his body plain enough in the cluttered rocks. He was a sitting target.

'Get down, f'chris'sake,' hissed Charlie uselessly across the space. He swallowed, wiped the sweat from his face, and eased his already aching body into a more comfortable position.

What now, he pondered? Darringo could play cat and mouse with them at will from here on, keep them held down for hours, days if he so chose. He could pick off a man whenever the mood took him. And would probably do just that, damn it.

He shifted, conscious of a movement at his side. McKee! 'Where the hell did you spring from?' he croaked, licking his lips.

'Never mind,' said McKee, settling himself at Charlie's side. 'We've got a problem here.'

'More than one, mister. You seen the state of that water. If we don't die from Darringo's lead, we'll sure as sun-up die of thirst.'

'Where's the next water?' asked McKee.

'Far side of Snake Pass. Day and a half's ride. A long way when you're thirsty.'

McKee grunted. 'You figure for Darringo still bein' here? Reckon he might have had his fill for one day?'

'Could be, I'd fancy for him wantin' to take us deeper, 'ceptin', o'course, he don't know who we are or why we're here. Unless he's recognized you. Could've spotted you back there on the track, and if that's the case . . . '

'I figure it,' murmured McKee. He gazed over the higher reaches for a moment, his concentration moving left to right, back again, stopping, inspecting as if turning aside a rock in search of the life beneath it. 'My bettin' is Darringo's already pulled out and moved on. But I'm goin' up there to see for m'self. Cover me best you can.'

'You want to take my gun? You're welcome.'

McKee tapped the hidden sheath beneath his shirt. 'Don't worry. I'll be fine. And if Rosen makes a move, keep him quiet. I don't want him or that sidekick Malone meddlin' where they ain't wanted.'

★   ★   ★

It was a long two hours through the searing afternoon heat before Charlie thought he had caught the merest glimpse of a shape moving through the shadows between ridge rocks. He could have been mistaken; might have been an animal, a low flying hawk, or worse, one of Darringo's men. But, no, he figured that McKee had made it and was still moving.

Did that mean he had found nothing, that the *bandidos* had pulled out, almost certainly heading for Snake Pass, or that he had seen plenty but had felt himself outnumbered?

'Hell's teeth!' Charlie had mouthed, wiping at yet another beading of sweat.

He moved round in the cover to get a clearer view of the track and the rocks where Rosen and his men were holed up. Thankfully, they had shown sense and stayed quiet. But for how much longer, wondered Charlie? Time would come when empty canteens and tightening thirsts would get the better of them, and then . . .

Charlie shrugged his shoulders. There would not be a drop of water taken from the pool at Eagle Point, much less drunk, not unless you were on a path hellbent to self-destruction. The pool was poisoned. Next stop: Snake Pass. How would Rosen take to that?

Charlie turned again, his gaze blood-shot now with the heat, the sun's blaze and the sheer effort of concentrating on the rocks.

'C'mon, McKee,' he murmured. 'Let's get this over with . . .'

★ ★ ★

It was over a half-hour later when, without warning, a slow trickle of stones and pebbles thickened to a cascade down the steep slope from the high rocks and, seconds later, a dead body followed in its wake.

Charlie was some minutes before he dared to move, straining his eyes to be certain that the tumbling heap of arms and legs and twisted body was, in fact, a *bandido* left behind as a lookout and not McKee.

It came to rest in a shower of scrub, stones and clouding dust and lay without moving in a suddenly spreading pool of blood.

'Goddamnit, he's done it,' hissed

Charlie, his eyes widening. 'Knifed,' he added flatly and with no surprise.

Twenty minutes later, Rosen, Malone and the remaining men were standing with Charlie and McKee at a respectful distance from the creek pool where now the water had developed a greasy yellow-streaked, bracken-coloured surface with a stench that pinched at the nostrils like grit.

'And so, Mr Roy, what now?' asked Rosen, with an ominous edge. 'I began this ride with a dozen men. I've lost six. We're darned near out of water, a long ways from the next source and — not puttin' too fine a point on it — at the mercy, it seems, of this scumbag Darringo. What do you recommend?'

'We could cut our losses and head back to Red Creeks,' said McKee, ahead of Charlie's sharp intake of breath. 'That would be good advice, 'ceptin' you won't be takin' it. Right?'

'Correct, Mr McKee.' Rosen thrust

his thumbs into his belt and stiffened his stance. 'Nothin's changed. I still want to bury my son's remains decent. You're leadin' me to where you left the body, for which I'm payin' you — and handsomely at that. What you choose to do *after* we have buried the body is mebbe goin' to be your affair, but I'm goin' on with the men I have left to kill Darringo. No messin'. Straight fact. I owe it to Johnny.'

'We're with you, Mr Rosen, you can trust to that,' leered Malone, dragging the cork from a bottle of whiskey.

Rosen eyed him with contempt for a moment, then continued, 'As for Mr Roy here, I value his worth as a scout through this territory, but I cannot compel him to go on if it's against his better judgement.'

'I gave my word to McKee. I ain't for quittin',' snapped Charlie, taking a grip of his unlit cherrywood.

Rosen nodded. 'Way I'm readin' the situation, it seems Darringo pulled out after that ambush, leavin' behind the single lookout Mr McKee has so effectively taken care of. My thanks for that.'

McKee stayed unmoved. Malone swigged at the whiskey bottle. The handful of men mopped their sweat-soaked necks. Charlie lit his pipe.

'Meanwhile,' Rosen went on, 'we have a serious water problem and some distance to cover before we reach another supply — assumin' Darringo doesn't get there ahead of us. So, Mr Roy, are we pullin' out and goin' on, or do I go alone?'

Charlie blew a thick cloud of smoke, waited for it to clear, then tightened his gaze on the track ahead. 'We go on,' he said bluntly. 'But there are rules. Water's goin' to have to be rationed 'til we reach Snake Pass. No laggin' behind; stay close; stay alert, but don't get jumpy. Darringo will figure soon enough where we're headin' and he may decide to hit us again. No sayin' for certain. But there'll be no easin' up, not if we're goin' to make it into safe cover by nightfall.' He blew another cloud of smoke. 'Let's bury these bodies. I ain't much for ridin' with the smell of death lingerin' back of me.'

11

Doc Whipple packed the last of his medical supplies into his saddle-bag, strapped it down, gave it a satisfied pat, and turned to face Sheriff Grove. 'Ready when you are — unless, of course, you've changed your mind.'

'No change, Doc,' said the sheriff, stepping to the edge of the dimly lit boardwalk fronting his office. He gazed over the steadily thinning night. 'Light will break in an hour. We'll pull out then.'

Doc nodded as Aaron Brewin grew out of the shadows. 'You fellas got all you need? You've only got to say. Store's open to you,' said the storekeeper.

'We'll be fine. Don't want to burden us too much,' grunted Grove. 'Got a feelin' it's goin' to be Doc's medical bag there that's goin' to be in demand,' he added darkly.

The three men stood in silence for a moment, their eyes probing the darkness, the emerging shapes, the faintest crease in the eastern skies.

'You reckon Marshal Keetch made the right choice?' murmured Brewin.

'I reckon,' said Doc. 'He's got to get to Rosen somehow, wherever he is. Find out just what it was pulled that son of his into the dirt.'

'Never doubted it,' said the sheriff. 'Keetch is a long-time lawman. He goes by the book, and this Johnny Rosen business ain't settled yet, leastways not by his reckonin'. I guess he's got to have some watertight proof of the fella's death; something definite he can take back to Pinecuts. Know how he feels. I'd be doin' exactly the same.'

'Ain't so sure about what you and Doc are doin', though,' said the storekeeper, lighting a cheroot. 'Ridin' into them mountains right now, what with Rosen huntin', Darringo prowlin', and now a marshal on the trail of both of them. A pretty potent mix, if you ask me.'

Grove yawned and stretched. 'Can't argue that, Aaron, but there ain't nobody in this town goin' to back off from lookin' to Charlie. So he might be crazy, more likely full of his own pride, but he's one on his own out there at his age.' He rolled his shoulders. 'I'll bring him in if it's the last thing I do, damn it!'

Brewin examined the glowing cheroot. 'Any number of men ready to ride with you, Sheriff,' he murmured. 'A dozen would come saddled up at the snap of my fingers.'

'Sure appreciate the concern, but Doc and me are keepin' this simple. A whole posse of riders hittin' them hills might be more trouble than they're worth. Besides we need you and the others to keep this old town of ours tickin' over.'

The men fell silent again as they watched Smoky O'Mara, cigar already lit and raising a head of smoke, cross the street from the saloon.

'Glad to see you fellas ain't pulled out yet,' he beamed, flicking ash to the street. 'I figured for both of you havin' a fittin' breakfast before you ride. So if you'd care to step across to the bar, gentlemen, the best I can offer awaits you. On the house!'

For some reason that was already taking the edge off Doc Whipple's appetite, he was thinking of the condemned man's last meal . . .

★ ★ ★

The darkness of night, the cooler air, had come as a welcome respite for Charlie and the riders. They had ridden almost without a break from the polluted water at Eagle Point on the treacherously difficult trail to Snake Pass. But they had progressed without further hindrance or attack from Darringo and the marauding *bandidos* — an absence that had itself been of concern.

'Don't like it,' Charlie had confided to McKee riding alongside him at the head of the bunch. 'Don't like it one bit. Too damned quiet.' He had spat fiercely. 'What the hell's Darringo plannin'? He ain't lettin' us move on for the benefit of our health. So mebbe he's waitin' til we make the Pass.' He grunted. 'We won't stand a snowflake in hell's chance if he hits us there.'

'Is there another way?' McKee had asked.

'Not unless you want to abandon your horse and climb hundreds of feet of razor-sharp rock.'

They had ridden on in silence for another mile before McKee drew his mount closer again. 'You notice anythin' particular back there at Eagle Point?'

'There was more than enough to be takin' in once I'd recovered from the shock of seein' the state of that water!' Charlie had quipped. 'But you ain't referrin' to the obvious, are you?'

McKee had frowned and pondered for a moment. 'Didn't strike me 'til I was up there in the rocks trackin' down that fella Darringo had left behind.' He had paused. 'How come, I got to wonderin', they only took out Rosen's sidekicks? How come they missed me, Rosen himself, and you? We were all easy targets. So why only the men?'

'Chance?' Charlie had shrugged. 'Some poor devil's bad luck?' He had shot a quick glance at McKee. 'You don't reckon so?'

'Well, mebbe. But I was for ponderin' on another possibility, pretty remote, but . . . Well, it was almost as if they had been ordered to take out only the men. As if they *knew* who we were. Or somebody did.'

And that had been another nagging concern for Charlie through the rest of that long, hot day to the approach of nightfall.

★   ★   ★

'How many men we got standin' guard, Mr Roy?' Edgar Rosen moved carefully into the full glow of the small fire in the rock clearing. 'Sufficient, I hope,' he added, a touch cynically.

'Same as I've always had posted at this stage on the trail,' said Charlie sharply, his eyes glinting in the thickening darkness. 'Just two. Don't call for more. 'Sides that's all we can spare right now.'

Rosen grunted and narrowed his gaze on the shadowy shapes of his sleeping men. 'Boys are all in. It's been a long day.'

'Yeah, well, if they think this has been rough goin', they ain't seen nothin' yet. And they'd best not go reckonin' for Darringo easin' up none.' Charlie packed the bowl of his cherrywood, held a taper to the fire, and let a slow cloud of tobacco smoke clear before he went on, 'No sayin' as to how many men he's brought in from across the border. I've known him hole-up in these mountains with as many as thirty, sometimes forty men. One thing's for certain, Mr Rosen, we're outnumbered, sure enough. Doin' battle with Darringo on level terms ain't never goin' to be the case.'

'Where's his main camp?' asked Rosen. 'Does he have one?'

'It shifts and moves around as he thinks fittin', and dependin' on who it is happens to be snappin' at his heels. Cloud Peak one day; three days later he's moved lock, stock and barrel to Rock Tor, or mebbe down to the Ridge. He don't give you no chance to pin him down.'

Rosen linked his hands behind his back and considered for a moment. 'Darringo seems to be holdin' the full deck and doin' all the dealin',' he said at last.

'You can bet to that, Mr Rosen. That's the way he prefers it. The *only* way in Darringo's book.'

They fell silent, their gazes wandering across the night, the shadows cast from the fire glow, the still sleeping shapes, the shifts here and there of moonlight as wispy cloud scudded on the first faint breezes. Charlie smoked thoughtfully. Rosen began to pace round the fire's edge, his steps measured, slow and careful.

It was a full five minutes before approaching steps through the loose stones and rocks alerted the two to the appearance of McKee. He paused at the sight of Charlie, glanced quickly at Rosen, then stepped into the full glow.

'Trouble?' asked Charlie, wafting aside the swirling pipe smoke. 'You seen somethin'?'

'That fella we posted guard top end of the hitch-line — he's dead,' said McKee softly. 'Throat's been cut. Darringo's men are that close.'

Rosen thought better of a string of curses, but broke into a cold sweat all the same as he stared first at McKee, then at Charlie.

'They touch the horses?' asked Charlie.

'We got lucky there,' said McKee. 'They left 'em.'

'Lucky be damned!' flared Charlie. 'Darringo wants us to ride on. He wants us to go deeper, the sonofabitch.' He thrust the glowing pipe into his mouth.

'You still for goin' on with this, Rosen?' said McKee, his gaze unblinking on the rancher's gleaming face.

'Like I said back there at the waterhole, nothin's changed, Mr McKee. We continue.'

'You're down to five men now,' murmured Charlie. 'The others ain't goin' to much like this when they wake.'

'They'll obey my orders,' snapped Rosen. 'I call all their shots — and they know it.'

''Ceptin' me,' drawled Malone, from the shadows ahead of the click of the hammer of his levelled Colt. 'I call all my shots myself, every last one.'

12

'I heard all that, every word, and for once the pipe-chewin' old-timer is right, the boys ain't goin' to like this, not one miserly bit.'

Malone's voice was surprisingly steady and level. 'They ain't goin' a stack on what happened earlier. They're goin' to be choked through at the thought of goin' on after this.' The Colt barrel glinted in the moonlight. 'Guess you're goin' to have to change your plans, Mr Rosen.'

'Not for you, Malone, not for anybody,' growled Rosen. 'And you can holster that piece, you drunken rat. Let me remind you — '

'No, let me remind you,' spat Malone. 'You can't make it through these goddamn mountains without me and the boys. None of you can. No chance. Minute Darringo hits us again, you're goin' to need all the guns you can level. T'ain't no use you relyin' on that old-timer there and a knife-throwin' drifter.' The Colt probed again. 'So I'd figure for you best wakin' up, Mr Rosen. Your son's dead; rottin' flesh, and not even you are big enough to face on to Darringo and his cut-throat *bandidos*. Let's call it a day, eh, and ride out while we're still drawin' breath?'

Charlie contemplated the fading glow in the bowl of his pipe. McKee stared at Malone and the glinting Colt like a snake watching its supper. Rosen sweated and seethed and would have launched himself into a tirade of cursing and maybe a physical attack on Malone had the levelled barrel ranged on his gut not been so steady. Malone was sober and deadly serious.

Charlie broke the stand-off in a calm, measured tone. 'Well, there ain't nobody goin' nowhere at this hour,' he said, tapping the ash from his pipe. 'So mebbe we should go cover the dead body out there and make sure we don't collect any more.'

McKee continued to stare, the fingers of his right hand flexing as if caught in the drift of a breeze.

Rosen grunted. 'Put that piece away, Malone,' he ordered. 'We ain't makin' any sense this way. We've got enough to look to with Darringo without gettin' to squabblin' among ourselves. Let's talk it through, eh, see if we can't — ?'

'We're with Malone,' came a voice from the shadows beyond the fire glow where the men were awake and watchful. 'We ain't goin' deeper, Mr Rosen. No point. We do that and we won't be comin' back, not any of us.'

Rosen broke into another beading of sweat as his lips twitched on hissed anger. 'I'll see the lot of you in hell!' he growled finally. 'You're cowards, and you'll not get another cent out of me 'til you come back to your senses. Not a cent, you hear?'

The Colt barrel glinted again as Malone's grip tightened. 'Mebbe you should've reckoned for all this when you gave that son of yours all the free rein you did.'

The words fell across the night like a handful of tossed stones. McKee stiffened and licked his lips. Charlie frowned.

Rosen's eyes narrowed to dark slits. 'What you sayin' there, Malone?'

'You know well enough what I'm sayin',' sneered Malone. 'Your only problem is you keep buryin' your head from the truth: that son of yours was a no-good, gamblin', boozin', womanizin' wastrel who probably got the death he deserved. And that's the fact of it. You're the only one who ain't seein' it. Time you woke up.'

The watching men murmured their support. McKee glanced quickly at Charlie, who tapped the bowl of his pipe thoughtfully in the palm of his hand. 'Somebody care to tell me what the hell's goin' on here?'

Malone sniggered. 'He don't know, does he? Nor does McKee there. You hear that, boys, Mr Rosen ain't bothered to tell our Red Creeks friends about his scumbag son! Now I wonder why? Strikes me you've got some explainin' to do.' The sidekick sniggered again. 'You goin' to get to it, Mr Rosen?'

'Hold it right there,' snapped Charlie, pocketing the pipe. 'I don't give a damn about Johnny Rosen right now. He don't figure none. Just let me remind you, the whole squabblin' lot of you, that one of your bunch is lyin' dead out there with his throat cut. And in case you ain't noticed — I posted two guards. Why is the other fella stayin' so quiet, and why ain't he joined us here? Hell, you've made enough noise to rouse him. So where is he?'

* * *

They found the second body sprawled in the rocks. He had been strangled, stripped of most of his clothing, his weapon, belt and boots, and shoved aside as if no more than a bundle of trash. His killers, probably numbering two, Charlie reckoned, had come and gone through the night like shadows. They had left nothing to indicate where they had come from or disappeared to.

'Typical,' said Charlie, staring at the body. 'That's Darringo for you. Put the whole deck back in our hands, ain't he? But deal it any way you like, our chances of goin' on and survivin' are shortenin'. Same can be said for gettin' out.'

'I say we pull out now,' clipped Malone, still with the Colt in his hand, as he eased back from the dead man to join the remaining men. 'Use the cover of night. Make all the distance we can before sun-up, and mebbe use the lesser known tracks. Goddamnit, there's gotta be some.'

'Oh, sure,' gestured Charlie. 'There's any number of remote tracks; tracks that ain't been used in years, 'ceptin' by animals; tracks that ain't felt so much as the scuff of boot leather or clip of a hoof in generations — and Darringo knows 'em all, every last one.'

'We're sittin' targets where we are,' voiced an ashen-faced sidekick, brushing the cold sweat from his stubble.

'Could be cold meat before dawn,' added another.

'Cut that talk, fella,' hissed Rosen, his gaze flaring as if lit suddenly. 'And holster that Colt, Malone, before you get to killin' somebody.' He glared while the man finally did as he was ordered. 'That's better,' said Rosen. 'And there'll be no more talk about Johnny. It ain't relevant. Right now we're still in the hands of Mr Roy and Mr McKee. And that is where we're stayin', and we're goin' on.'

Malone spat. The men murmured and shuffled uncomfortably. McKee eased the tightness of his hat.

'Any which way you go is all the same right now,' said Charlie. 'It don't matter. Darringo's goin' to be there, anyhow, and there ain't a darned thing we can do about it . . . '

It was to be another ten minutes,

with the fire rebuilt and the flames dancing briskly, the men gathered round it, some smoking, some conversing in low, muttered tones, before anybody noticed that McKee was missing.

He, too, had disappeared like a shadow.

★　★　★

Marshall Jim Keetch winced through clenched teeth as he shifted uncomfortably in his seat in the rocks, blinked his sore eyes and wished once again he had made the sensible choice and headed back to Pinecuts.

But he knew also that he was lying to himself.

He would no more have given up the hunt for Johnny Rosen, dead or alive, than he would think of throwing in his law badge. The heinous shooting and rape at the Scott homestead had been too brutal, too bloodthirsty to be passed over on the say-so of one man discovering a body in the mountains.

Keetch wanted more — another witness — maybe a sight of the body or what remained of it, the word of Darringo or one of his *bandidos*, but more than that he wanted to face Edgar Rosen, to tell him down to the last miserable detail what he had found that day at the homestead. Watch his face as he heard it; make him smell it . . .

He winced again at the sharpness of the rocks. It was full night now, but he had made fast progress out of Red Creeks and hit the mountains well before darkness had closed in.

Tomorrow, he would leave the main trail and climb higher using the little known tracks where a single rider and mount could save miles in reaching the heart of these lands. He would be hoping for a sight of Darringo or maybe picking up Rosen's progress with the scout Charlie Roy.

And there was another fellow intriguing him, one by the name of McKee.

Keetch had heard tell of such a man who travelled with only knives as his weapons, who could aim and hurl a blade faster than a man could draw and blaze a sidearm.

They had known nothing of the man or his reputation back at Red Creeks, nor it seemed had Rosen.

But Darringo had seen him at work. What had he reckoned to such a man crossing his mountains? More to the point, what would he be figuring now that the man had returned?

13

It had needed no more than the softest break in the covering of night cloud, the merest shimmer of first light in the east for the party to be mounted up and readied for the trek deeper into Snake Pass.

Charlie rode with McKee at his elbow. 'You gave me one almighty scare back there,' murmured the scout, beyond the earshot of Rosen and the others. 'Where'd you disappear to, f'chris'sake?'

'Took a look round,' said McKee quietly, his hands easy on the reins, his gaze scanning the rocks and higher peaks. 'There's about eight of Darringo's men keepin' watch on us. I figure mebbe evenly split: four trackin' our rear, four ahead of us. No horses. They're movin' on foot.'

'And that suggests Darringo's close.

I'd reckon for him holdin' a larger band of men and waitin' horses for the men on foot far end of the pass.' Charlie had rummaged for his pipe but left it unlit.

'Could be that's where he'll hit us big time,' said McKee.

'Mebbe, mebbe,' pondered Charlie. 'But I still ain't seen anythin' that really shows his hand. Like you say, he's bein' selective in who he takes out — and that foxes me some.'

'Figures on takin' hostages for ransom?' asked McKee.

'He's done it before, sure enough,' answered Charlie. 'But he usually favours takin' women when they're available. They fetch a higher price and provide his entertainment while he's waitin' on the payout. Darringo don't believe in wastin' anythin'.' He was silent for a moment. 'He'd have to know who Rosen is and of his wealth to make a ransom heist worthwhile. And he don't, does he?'

But for Charlie and McKee there were other more pressing problems to occupy their thoughts as they made their slow, silent way through the breaking shafts of early light.

Just what, for instance, had Malone been on the verge of telling of the real Johnny Rosen and his seemingly wasteful past? Had he some personal axe of envy to grind against the rancher's son, or had Johnny indeed been the high-living, free-spinning wastrel he had suggested? And how had that, if it were true, brought the young man into these mountains to a death at the hands of Juan Darringo?

There was, too, the increasing difficulty of Malone. Both Charlie and McKee had recognized the venom in the collapsing relationship between the hired hand and his boss. Malone appeared now to have the support and following of Rosen's men, or those left of the original dozen, but his mood and the constant threat of his drunkenness made for a powder-keg waiting to be lit.

And when and where would that be, Charlie had pondered more than once.

Maybe there was something to be said for heaving this whole heap of trouble aside and making the break back to that shady veranda and the comfort of the rocker. But not now and probably not this day, he mused, as McKee drew his attention to the glint of a rifle barrel high in the light dappled rocks.

'And we were meant to see that,' he had added ruefully.

★　★　★

Sheriff Grove and Doc Whipple had been careful in the plotting of their trek into the mountains and worked on a possible route some hours before finally pulling out of Red Creeks.

'Just bein' the two of us makes one hell of a difference,' Grove had said, examining the old map spread across his desk. 'Means we can maybe avoid the main trail in parts and cut into the narrower tracks. Marshal Keetch will be figurin' the same but I've got my own ideas . . .'

Grove's main strategy had been a first thrust into the foothills further to the east, thus avoiding, he reckoned, the difficulties of negotiating Eagle Point and much of the darker, deeper and more dangerous approaches of Snake Pass.

'Been some years since I trailed the mountains with any serious intent, so I'm mebbe goin' to flounder some, but I'm reckonin' on Long Ridge bein' where we'll find Charlie and the rest of 'em. God willin'. So, the eastern foothills it is. Tough goin' out there . . .'

Tough going had been an understatement. Dense, thickly coated slopes of ancient pine and clinging scrub and brush had at first seemed an impenetrable barrier.

'Hell's feet, seems like the place just don't want us!' had been Doc's verdict, an hour into the struggle.

But they had persisted, hand trailing their mounts round fallen trees and the twisted debris of branches, skirting near head high walls of scrambling creepers and whipping brush, skids of loose rocks and shale and, here and there, the tumbling outflows of creek streams.

They had never been entirely sure of the hour, such was the density of the overhead canopy with only the occasional break for the light to penetrate.

Doc had lost track of time when they finally struggled the last few yards to the top of the slopes and breathed the cleaner, fresher air of the mountains.

'And amen to that!' the sheriff had pronounced, mopping his scratched, dusty face. 'There'll just have to be an easier way down!'

But all that, thought Doc, would depend on the next few hours of the new day dawning and what it might hold.

★   ★   ★

'I get the distinct feelin' we're bein' watched,' hissed Rosen at Charlie's back. 'Would I be right, Mr Roy?'

'You'd be better than right, Mr

Rosen,' said Charlie. 'You'd be dead-eyed spot on!'

Rosen grunted quietly. 'Figured so. More than one of 'em up there. Counted a half-dozen at least.'

'And they're only lookouts. Main party will be gathered a mile or so on.'

'So do we rein up, Mr Roy?' asked Rosen. 'Or do we walk into whatever's awaitin' us?'

'Please yourself,' said Charlie. 'If we rein up, so will they. If we turn back, they'll follow. If we go on . . . You get the picture?'

'No choice,' grunted Rosen.

'Precisely.'

The rancher was silent for a moment before beginning again: 'Might not this be the time to try some sort of negotiations with Darringo?'

'That's what me and Mr McKee have been reckonin', but not 'til we're approachin' the ridge where McKee covered the body. Then we rein up; then we wait, and then we get to talkin', assumin' Darringo's in the mood.'

'And what are the chances of that?'

Charlie pondered thoughtfully. 'Well, put it this way, Mr Rosen, if I were a gamblin' man asked to wager on them odds, I'd not only be lookin' for a means of closin' down on the game, I'd be scoutin' for the quickest way out of the room!'

* * *

The party trailed on for another hour, their eyes never leaving the sheer rock walls of the pass as they rode ever deeper into the engulfing closeness. The light now was full, but no more than a graveyard of shadows in the depths of the pass, the air strangely chilled as if ghosts had breathed there through the night. Sounds echoed eerily; voices stayed muted; words were not necessary in such a place: there was nothing to be said.

'You recall this part of the trail, Mr McKee?' murmured Charlie at the man's side.

'It's familiar,' answered McKee.

'Far to go?'

'Half-mile at the most. I'll lead when I'm certain.'

'Be my guest,' said Charlie. 'I'll keep watch on the rats up there. I'd give a whole heap now to know their game. Any notions?'

'None. They could have taken us anytime they wanted. I don't get it.'

'Me neither,' sighed Charlie, 'so we'll just keep right on goin' . . . '

The half-mile came and went, and it was some distance on before McKee raised an arm and indicated a track through a narrow passage in the wall to his left.

They passed through in single file, McKee leading, followed by Charlie and Rosen with Malone and the others bringing up the rear. No one spoke; the pace was easy on the clip of hoofs, the gentle creak of leather and jangle of tack.

McKee stayed concentrated, recalling the day he had seen the high hawk circling overhead, heard its call, watched it swoop to the ledge above the body, the day Darringo and his *bandidos* had come within a whisker of taking his life and leaving him dead in the rocks for the buzzards to pick his bones clean.

They broke through the passage and into the rock and boulder-strewn open like a column of ants.

'This it? This where you found Johnny?' asked Rosen, shielding his eyes against the sudden glare of sunlight.

'Over there,' said McKee, already slipping clear of the saddle.

'The rest of you stay mounted,' ordered Charlie.

'Leave this to McKee.'

They stared, tense and in silence as they watched McKee thread his slow way through and over the rocks to the shadowy depths of a bulging boulder. A horse snorted. A hoof clipped rock. A man spat. Rosen sweated and swallowed. Malone's eyes narrowed. Charlie's gaze moved steadily over the higher rocks, watchful for the glint of a barrel, the shift of a shadow.

'Well,' said Rosen again, 'what can you see? Is the body there, damnit?'

'Patience, Mr Rosen,' murmured Charlie. 'Fella's doin' his best.'

McKee moved on, step by measured step, picking his way like a crab. He paused a moment, reached for a bandanna to mop his sweat-stained face and brow, gazed into the cloudless blue sky almost expecting to see the hawk. There was nothing. He wiped the band of his hat, settled himself to a new balance and pushed on, the memories of carting the body to its final resting place that day, the sudden crack of a voice across the shimmering heat flooding back eerily.

'Hey, gringo, it's you again, the blade man! So you've come back to settle things with Darringo, eh? How about that? You're a bigger fool than I took you for!'

The men, Rosen, Charlie and Malone had frozen where they sat their mounts in stunned silence at the sudden snap of

Darringo's voice through the thickening morning air.

McKee halted, hardly able to believe what he was seeing as he stared at the same pot-bellied figure straddling the rocky ledge above him, the bandoleer across his chest gleaming in the sunlight, his eyes still as black, the glare as harsh, penetrating and vicious as ever.

The bandit-leader's deep belly laugh set the layers of fat at his waist rolling like waves to a shore. 'Hey, gringo, what's with all the faces?' he bellowed into the echoes of his laughter. 'This your private army, eh? Your friends? Aren't you goin' to introduce 'em before I get a second chance to kill you?'

14

'Don't nobody take a breath that ain't necessary,' hissed Charlie, his gaze fixed like a beam on Darringo's face. 'That rat'll shoot you soon as spit.'

'We're surrounded,' added Rosen, in a similarly hissed breath. 'There's rifles gleamin' everywhere.'

'T'ain't escaped my notice, Mr Rosen. That's why we don't move a muscle. Them *bandidos* have got nothin' to lose.'

Malone hawked and spat. A horse shook its head against a pestering fly, the jangle of tack echoing thinly above the walls of rock. The sidekicks shifted uncomfortably, but stayed silent and watchful, not daring to so much as run their fingers through the hot, sticky reins.

'Still as talkative as ever I see,' grinned Darringo laconically, flicking at the rim of his vast sombrero. 'You fellas get anythin' out of this gringo, my friends?' he asked, directing his black gaze over Charlie, Rosen and Malone.

Rosen made to speak, but was restrained by Charlie.

'I could take him out as easy as blinkin',' mouthed Rosen.

'And leave us all for the buzzards!' quipped Charlie, on a withering glance.

McKee advanced a step. 'Fella back here is Mr Edgar Rosen, of Montana,' he called. 'You robbed and shot his son, Johnny — the body I found and covered right here. Mr Rosen's come a long ways to collect Johnny's remains and see them buried decent.'

Darringo's fingers drummed idly across the thick leather belt at his waist. He gestured sharply to someone unseen to his right, spoke quickly in a guttural spurt of Spanish to a man at his back, and settled a broad, tooth-filled grin on McKee.

'I am touched, my friend,' he said, flicking again at the brim of the sombrero. 'It is good that a father should wish to see his son buried decent. I know these things. I feel them. I am a father many, many times! Too many sons to count now, eh? All my men are my sons.'

He tittered until the sweat was beading like silver dust through his stubble and across his cheeks. 'But I can do better than let the gringo there collect the bones of his son,' Darringo began again. 'Oh, yes, my friend, I most certainly can.' He raised his arms. 'Juan Darringo is a worker of miracles!'

He stood aside to let a tall, lean, clean-shaven, well-dressed young fellow step from behind him into the full glare of the sunlight.

'You see, gringo,' he beamed, his white teeth flashing. 'I give you Johnny Rosen, the man you have come to bury, alive and well!'

* * *

There was a long silence in which nothing moved or seemed to have a life, as if the moment had been stripped and was balancing barefoot on the sharp ends of pins.

McKee did nothing save to hold his position in the rocks and full glare of the searing sunlight and stare at Darringo and the man at his side.

Edgar Rosen's mouth had dropped open, his eyes widened, his skin turned a ghostly ashen, his thoughts sent spinning. 'Johnny,' was all he could croak.

The sidekicks' gasps had come as if from one body. Only Malone, his gaze narrowing, a frown deepening across his brow, had found words at the back of a suddenly dusty throat. 'It's him. No mistakin'. That's Johnny Rosen.'

It had been left to Charlie to watch for what was developing round them as the *bandidos* moved out of cover and circled the mounted men, their rifles levelled, their dark eyes mean and unblinking.

'Just what the hell is happenin' here?' growled Rosen at last, snapping out of his trance. 'What in the name of sanity are you doin' here? How come you're with this thievin' outfit? You're supposed to be dead, goddamnit! So who's the body under them rocks, and just what in tarnation — ?'

Darringo's rifle blazed two fast shots high into the heat-laden air. 'Enough,' he shouted, stepping to the edge of the ledge to glare down on McKee and the riders. 'There'll be no more talk. Not here. You will come with me — everybody, except the gringos over there.' He pointed to the men mounted behind Malone.

'Now you hold on there, mister,' blustered Rosen, shifting his gaze from his son to Darringo. 'They're my men, on my payroll. I say what they do, where they go, and don't you f'get it. You may run your outfit any old how you think fittin', but in my part of the world we do things by the book — *my* book! So you'll lay off orderin' my men around, mister, you've done enough damage already, and I'll see you in hell for that before — '

Rosen, McKee, Charlie and Malone swung round as the *bandidos*' rifles roared in unison in a hail of fire that threw the remaining ranch hands from their saddles and left them lifeless in merging pools of blood.

'And that, Señor Rosen, is my book,' grinned Darringo, his face gleaming in a lathering of sweat. 'I read it my way.' He laughed until the echoes lifted hawks and buzzards from their perches. 'And now bring on the scavengers! They will have a banquet! As for you, gringos, you will hand your weapons to my men and follow me in silence. First gringo to speak is a dead gringo. And Darringo does not joke!'

* * *

Marshall Keetch had been making steady progress when the distant gunfire deep in the mountainous folds of rock and stone towards Long Ridge had shattered the silence of the hot morning.

He had reined up sharply, dropped a hand instinctively to his holstered Colt, and peered ahead as if expecting gunmen to materialize like ghosts through the shimmering heat-haze. He watched as three buzzards took to the air like black smudges, saw them climb, wheel, and then begin a slow, drifting return to their rocky havens — or maybe, they were feeding grounds by now.

The echoes of the gunfire faded, the morning slipped back to sun and silence, heat and scorching rocks, and Keetch relaxed. Darringo's men out there, sure to be, he decided. But who or what had been their targets? Rosen and his party? It was unlikely that any other body of men had taken recently to the mountain tracks.

He flicked the reins for the mount to walk on, and pondered his next move. He would need to go with extra care from here on as he searched for wherever Darringo had his current lair.

He rode on, easing the mount along the narrow track, his thoughts already racing on the sounds of the gunshots and what they might mean. Maybe he had gotten lucky and was closer to Darringo and his men than he had figured likely at this stage. But maybe Rosen, McKee, Charlie Roy and the others had not been so fortunate. Maybe they had caught the full blast of the bandit leader's cruel anger.

It might only be a matter of hours now before he found out . . .

At about the same time that Marshall Keetch had reined up at the crack of gunfire and watched the circling buzzards, Doc Whipple and Sheriff Grove had risked the telltale curl of smoke from a small fire in pursuit of the comforts of fresh, hot coffee.

They had been in need of it after the tough climb through the foothills, they had decided. But steaming mugs had stayed cupped in hands at the crack of the shots miles to the east of where they had reached and somewhere, Doc later figured, on the fringes of Long Ridge.

'Darringo,' had been the first word to pass the sheriff's lips.

'Charlie and his party,' Doc had followed, staring into the sunlit distances.

'You reckon for Darringo havin' hit them?' asked Grove some minutes after the muffled echoes had faded.

'I reckon,' croaked Doc. 'Them shots were definitely from the direction of the ridge, and that was Charlie's first destination. Reach the ridge, locate the body of Johnny Rosen and get the hell out while they were still breathin'. That had been the plan, but maybe Darringo and his pack had been ahead of them all along.'

'We should push on fast,' said Grove. 'Try to link up with Keetch.' He had fallen gravely silent for a moment. 'If Darringo's taken prisoners for his own amusement, I wouldn't give a handful of dirt for their chances.'

They had only sipped at their coffee

131

before finally throwing it aside, killing the fire, mounting up and pushing on down the mountain track.

They had no taste for much else.

★ ★ ★

Charlie Roy eased to the slow, rolling pace of his horse, his mind on fire, his thoughts a cluttered mayhem, his gaze anywhere but where he seemed to be, somewhere in the cavernous creeks and cuts of the Long Ridge. Nor was he conscious of where Darringo and the *bandidos* were leading him and the stunned remnants of the party that had left Red Creeks. Perhaps right now he did not care. The world had gone stark raving mad and was stalked by the ghosts of men supposedly dead and now alive. If they were.

He blinked, shook the sweat from his face and tried desperately for a moment to think straight.

Rosen's men, with the exception of Malone, were all dead, taken out in cold blood. Fact. No going back on that. Johnny Rosen was alive. Fact. Rosen had confirmed it had been his son standing there on the ledge at Darringo's side. How the man had survived and come to be there was, for now, unknown. Fact.

Charlie blinked again. Darringo was in control and, surprisingly for a man not known for any generosity, had taken prisoners. Fact. What nobody knew was what he had planned for them, when or how or precisely where. But Charlie could hazard pretty accurate guesses on all three counts. And you might call that brutal fact.

But was Johnny Rosen going to stand by and watch his father humiliated and then cruelly murdered?

How was McKee going to react? His knives had been taken from him and he was as weapon-naked as the rest. Would he plot an escape? But how in hell was anyone ever going to communicate with him?

And what of Malone? How long

before his short fuse finally blew him apart?

Would Sheriff Grove hold to his word and send out a search party? How long before he did? Hell, it might take days for riders to find them. Fact.

Charlie swallowed and tried to concentrate as best he was able on the track ahead and where Darringo was leading them.

They were moving ever deeper into a creek or long gulch. Would this be Darringo's current camp? Very likely, thought Charlie. It would be well hidden, with a supply of fresh water, dry caves and approachable from only one side which would be heavily guarded day and night by men who shot first and never asked questions. Once within the rocky prison there would be no getting out, leastways not alive.

And that was the harshest fact.

15

Marshal Keetch had ridden into the path of Sheriff Grove and Doc Whipple almost by accident. There had been no untoward sounds, no contact by sight by any of the parties, nothing until two narrow mountain tracks had converged in the shadows of boulders and Keetch was suddenly facing a bemused Sheriff Grove and a smiling Doc Whipple.

'It's true what they say about these darned mountains,' Doc had grinned, 'you just never know what's round the next rock!'

'Or in the case of some of the scum out here, what you might find under one!' the sheriff had added ruefully.

The three men had quickly exchanged accounts of their progress since leaving Red Creeks, and agreed without much doubt that the gunfire they had all heard earlier was from Darringo's men.

'Them were repeatin' rifles blazin' away,' Keetch had deduced. 'Just the sort of weapons Darringo would favour. That was him out there, all right, you can bet to it.'

'What we don't know,' the sheriff had said, sharing his canteen with Doc, 'is how many are still in the party Charlie led out of Red Creeks, if they'd lost men before this mornin's encounter, and what's happened to them since.'

'But we can make a fair stab at an accurate guess,' Doc had murmured darkly. 'They've been taken, or wiped out. One or the other. Gunfire didn't last long enough for it to be a battle of any kind. No, my figurin' would be that Darringo bushwhacked Charlie and his party somewhere near Long Ridge, had the upper hand from the outset, and either finished it right there in one godalmighty massacre, or took prisoners. No splittin' hairs over it.'

'Reckon you're about right, Doc,' the marshal had agreed. 'So where does that leave us?

'With no choice by my reckonin', the sheriff had been quick to add. 'We go on. We've got to know what's happened. If it's a massacre, we do the decent thing by the bodies. If it ain't — '

'It ain't no massacre,' Doc had chipped in. 'I just got that feelin' back of this old neck here. I just can't see men like Charlie Roy and that fella McKee comin' to that sort of end. T'ain't in their nature. So I'm figurin' for them bein' prisoners along of whoever is still standin'.' He paused thoughtfully for a moment. 'How long they'll stay prisoners is mebbe another matter. I don't figure Darringo goin' much on the cagin' of prisoners for longer than their worth — which means we ain't got long.'

The three men had fallen into silence, their gazes ranging slowly over the hills and mountains, the twists of scrub and brush, the piles and drifts of rock and the thousand crevices, creeks and hidden gulches they might hide from the eyes of men and their mounts.

They watched the silent soaring of an eagle, its moment of seeming to lay on the air like something painted there, the gentle circling, the wheeling out of sight behind a jutting crag.

Keetch's mount snorted and shook its head against the persistence of an arrogant fly.

'Let's move out,' said the marshal at last. 'Should make Snake Pass and the lower reaches of Long Ridge well before sundown.' He flicked at the reins. 'We're three guns against — '

'A hidin' to nothin'!' grinned Doc. 'But mebbe that's our advantage.'

★   ★   ★

They were into and negotiating Snake Pass by the late afternoon. The light was still bright, the sun still fierce though already beginning its slow descent in the western skies, and the air through the shadowed eeriness and silence of the pass cooler and thinner.

'We keep our eyes peeled from here on,' the Marshal had murmured before taking point in the single file approach. 'We've no idea where Darringo might be holed up. It could be anywhere. But there might be a clue: some print in what sand there is; a distant sound; anythin'. We don't miss nothin'.'

But nothing was precisely what could not be missed, thought Doc, his eyes concentrated as much on the ground being covered as on the towering walls of the pass. And just when, he was also pondering, had Darringo's look-outs first spotted them? Surely they were up there somewhere, had to be. That was the whole essence of the bandit leader's lawless strategy: know who is approaching before they have the time to take a first gulp of mountain air.

He voiced his fears to Sheriff Grove riding ahead of him. 'You see anythin'?' he hissed. 'Any of Darringo's scum?'

'Nothin' yet,' Grove had answered. 'Mebbe they're all restin' up.'

'Yeah, and mebbe rattlers are cosyin'

up to rats!' quipped Doc. 'I figure for somebody bein' up there. Wouldn't be natural otherwise.'

But they had trailed on slowly, the mounts down to a walking pace as the sheer walls of rock seemed to close in. Doc's eyes were already aching under the strain of his concentration. Grove had cleared the sweat a dozen times from his gaze as it roved from the surface rocks and sand to the jagged outline of summits etched against the glow of the gathering evening light.

It was Keetch who saw the empty bottle first.

★　★　★

'Malone's doin',' said Doc, slipping from the saddle to join the marshal and Sheriff Grove where they stood staring at the discarded empty whiskey bottle. 'He was lucky it fell into sand. If Darringo's boys had heard it smash on rocks, they'd probably have shot him.'

'Proves the party came this way,

anyhow,' said Grove.

'Proves *one* of the party came this way,' murmured Doc.

Their gazes moved round the area, the jumbled rocks, stone and sand of the trail's surface, the smooth walls of the pass reaching to heights far above them, and then to the narrow passage some yards ahead that disappeared into the darker depths of whatever creek or gulch lay beyond.

'Through there,' said Keetch, pointing to the cut.

'That might figure some,' pondered Doc, rubbing his chin. 'I'd reckon for a whole maze of creeks stretchin' the other side of these rock faces. No sayin' how many or how deep. We goin' to take a look?'

'Best if only one of us takes a first look,' said Keetch. 'I'll go, see what there is to see, and if it looks promisin' I'll come back for you. It'll be safer if I approach on foot.'

'Well, go easy and get back the minute you've got somethin' positive,' said Grove. 'If it is that Darringo's got a camp somewhere in there, we ain't for walkin' into it. And keep your eyes skinned for look-outs. He's certain to have posted them.'

'Good luck,' grunted Doc, taking the reins of the marshal's mount. He was a little while before he added to Keetch's back: 'You're goin' to need it.'

* * *

Charlie Roy shifted as close to the mouth of the cave as he thought prudent under the scowling glares of the guard, and took in what he could see of Darringo's lair.

A large flat area at the centre of a bowl-shaped canyon of smooth rock faces and jagged crags; cooking utensils scattered round the central fire; blankets, barrels, boxes; a handful of raven-haired, dark-eyed women moving silently from caves to the fire, some to a tub where an older woman dealt with a pile of dirty washing; a line of loose-hitched horses and ponies; men resting, relaxing, dozing in the few areas of shade, and high among the rocks above the entrance to the bowl the inevitable guards patrolling back and forth like lions ready to pounce on anything that moved. Nothing to be seen of Darringo or Edgar Rosen and his son.

Charlie was conscious of McKee at his elbow. 'Darn near to bein' a fortress,' whispered the man. 'Darringo's been here some time.'

'This place is as good as permanent,' murmured Charlie. He wiped a lathering of sweat from his face. 'Just wish I knew what the hell's goin' on. Where's Darringo? What's happened to Rosen, and just what in the name of sanity is his son doin' here? Whole thing's about as tangled as a mangrove swamp. You figured it?'

'Not yet I ain't,' hissed McKee. 'But I've got one helluva feelin' we've been duped down to our boots.'

Charlie sighed. 'What about Malone?'

'Would you believe, sleepin' it off back of the cave there!'

'Not surprisin'. He'd finished a whole bottle of Smoky O'Mara's best whiskey before we got here. Man's an idiot.'

'What happened to the bottle?' asked McKee.

'The what?' frowned Charlie.

'The bottle? What happened to the empty bottle? What did Malone do with it?'

Charlie stared long and hard into McKee's eyes. 'Yeah,' he murmured almost to himself, his mind already spinning through a dozen thoughts. 'Just what did happen to that bottle?'

The scowling guard crossed to the side of the cave, banged the barrel of his rifle on the rock, and glared at his captives. 'Darringo's comin',' he growled.

16

Juan Darringo was shorter and rounder at close quarters, a dark, swarthy-skinned man with glaring eyes, flared nostrils, wet lips and flashing teeth. The sweat on his stubble and matted black hair glistened like a scattering of ice. A bandoleer at his chest was full and heavy. He packed a holstered Colt to his right, a sheathed knife to his left. A sombrero hung loose at his back.

A grin spread at his thick lips until he was deep into a belly laugh. 'So, you have come back, gringo?' he smiled, addressing McKee. 'You have saved me a lot of time and trouble.' The smile faded. 'Now I can kill you at my leisure. Slowly.'

He turned to Charlie. 'And you, I am told, are a one-time mountain scout in the employ at the moment of Señor Rosen. Perhaps I can use you, eh?'

'Like the hell you will!' snapped Charlie. 'I wouldn't — '

'Save your breath,' growled Darringo. 'You may not have too much of it left.'

'Where's Rosen?' asked McKee bluntly. 'And just what is his son doin' here?'

Darringo spat across the cave floor. 'Ah, yes, of course,' he smiled again. 'The silver chain. It confused you, eh, gringo?'

McKee's eyes narrowed. 'Johnny Rosen was here with you, on the day I found the body?' he asked.

'But, of course. Señor Rosen has been with me for some time now. What you found was Johnny Rosen's chain and one of his unfortunate compatriots. He served a useful purpose. Sadly the other gringo who accompanied Johnny here has also since met with an accident.' Darringo shrugged. 'Who cares? Life is cheap in the mountains, eh, Señor Roy? You would know that better than most.'

Charlie merely stared and seethed quietly.

'You holdin' Johnny Rosen prisoner? A hostage?' croaked McKee, on a dry, dusty throat.

'Nothing so crude, gringo,' grinned Darringo. 'Johnny Rosen is with me, one of my group. A *bandido*.' He tapped the side of his bulbous nose with a stiff fore-finger. 'He is one bad gringo. Do you know that, *señors*? Oh, yes, one very bad gringo. A wanted man, *señors*, who has found his true self and refuge right here with me in my mountains.'

'His pa might have somethin' to say about that,' grunted Charlie.

'But, of course,' gestured Darringo expansively. 'He has already been told the deal we are proposing.' The man's smile seemed to bubble up through his wet lips. 'He will pay and pay handsomely for his son to remain in my protection. Oh, yes, make no mistake. He has — how do you say? — already got the drift. You follow, *señors*?'

'Blackmail,' clipped Charlie.

'And Johnny's goin' along with this?' said McKee.

'Naturally. Johnny Rosen is no Montana rancher, *señor*. He is a born *bandido* — fearless, ruthless, living for today with no thought for what has been and little for what may or may not come to be.'

Darringo gazed beyond McKee and Charlie to the slumped, sleeping form of Raps Malone. 'Get him,' he ordered the guard. 'It is time we had some entertainment!'

★　★　★

Marshal Keetch stood perfectly still. One false move now, a sharper intake of breath, the shift of a boot, slip on so much as a pebble, and the rattler would strike.

He swallowed, sweated, stared at the snake and willed it to move on, slide like a shadow across the sand to the cover of rocks, and disappear. But it was to be another gruelling two minutes before the rattler turned its attention to a patch of shade some distance behind Keetch, and made for it at speed.

The marshal sighed, relaxed, mopped the beaded sweat from his face and tightened his gaze on the passage ahead. He had moved quickly, silently since leaving Doc Whipple and the sheriff in the pass. There had been no hint so far of Darringo's patrolling guards on the higher reaches of the smooth rock faces, but they were there, you could bet to it.

But for now, with the rattler safely behind him, the light still good and the silence encouraging, he would push on to discover what he could of where the passage led.

He stepped quietly, carefully through the rocks and sand, hugging the deeper shadows and the sheer walls wherever he could. There was no evidence, he noted, of riders having passed this way recently. Or had Darringo had someone cover the tracks?

He paused a moment, mopped his face again, and squinted into the streaks and patches of light high above him. Still no hint of patrolling guards. Still no sounds. He grunted to his thoughts. Maybe he and Doc and the sheriff had got it wrong. Maybe the empty bottle had simply been dropped, thrown down and Charlie Roy and his party ridden on. Maybe he was wasting his time here.

And then a horse snorted.

He tensed, slid a hand to the butt of his holstered Colt, and peered ahead to where the sound had seemed to hang on the air. How close, he wondered? A rider heading down the passage towards him? The snort of a hitched mount? Where was its rider?

He waited, listening, his eyes flitting from shadows to shapes, rocks to stones. Then he moved, quickly now, covering the ground with long strides, his Colt drawn. He flattened himself against the rocks as the light ahead grew from no more than a pale sliver to a brighter glare, widening and strengthening.

He halted again, took a firmer grip on the Colt, swallowed and covered the last few yards to the edge of the glare without pausing.

The narrow passage had opened like a mouth on a bowl-shaped clearing, very obviously an encampment from the scatterings of possessions and activity he could make out. The sides of the bowl were dotted with dark, brooding caves.

He backed to a patch of deeper shadows, his gaze fixing on the line of hitched mounts, not all of them *bandidos'* horses, he reckoned. Some of the better-looking mounts were well fed and cared for ranch and town stock.

He instinctively dropped to one knee at the sound of a voice calling in Spanish. An echoing reply drifted from high above him. No question now, he decided, he had reached Darringo's lair, and would wager a month's pay that somewhere, maybe in any of the dozen caves he could see, Charlie Roy, Edgar Rosen, McKee and whoever of the party had survived so far, were being held prisoner.

But what would be the chances of a bid to free them? Slim, if he were honest, he thought, squinting again into the glare as the voices and hitched mounts fell silent. And no time either to raise help, leastways not before Darringo had decided the fate of his captives once his patience with them had been exhausted.

He swallowed again on a throat that was tight with tension and as dry as the dust and dirt at his boots. Had McKee found the body of Johnny Rosen, he wondered, or had the bandits been waiting on the party reaching Long Ridge and ambushed them?

The marshal grunted quietly. He needed to talk with Edgar Rosen, to establish once and for all just what — '

He had heard nothing, not a breath, not a football; seen nothing of the lengthening shadow or the shape behind it. And it was all too late when his mind finally cleared of questions and he heard the chilling click of a gun hammer at his back.

'Drop the weapon and walk ahead,' ordered the greasy voice. 'And do not turn round, not if you want to take another breath.'

17

'So what do we do: Stay put, push on down the pass, or go see just where in hell that marshal's gotten himself?' Doc Whipple's eyes gleamed through the shadow of the rock face where he sat his mount. 'Don't see as how we have a deal of choice.'

'None,' said Sheriff Grove bluntly, a hand raised to shield his eyes against the glare of the sun. 'T'ain't goin' to be more than an hour or so before the light begins to fade. I'm for stayin' put awhiles, give ourselves some evening cover before we start probin' too deep.'

'You figure for Keetch havin' found somethin'? Mebbe Darringo is holed up back of these rocks.'

'He's found somethin', or seen somethin',' said Grove, 'otherwise he'd have been back by now.' He narrowed his gaze on the entrance to the passage, the brooding walls of the high rocks, the already lengthening shadows as the sun began its descent in the west. 'It's the silence I don't like,' he murmured.

'Me neither,' agreed Doc, his gaze roving along the drift of the pass. He continued to gaze and concentrate for a moment. 'It's a long shot, I know, but I've just got the feelin' . . . ' He eased his mount a step forward from the shadow. 'There's a track up from the floor of the pass to the top of the rocks there. See . . . ' He pointed and traced the fissure and narrow track following it to the higher reaches. 'I reckon if I — '

'That's no place for a man of your age, Doc,' clipped Grove, concentrating his own gaze on the track. 'And I ain't for havin' you riskin' your chances on a climb like that, but I get your meanin': if somebody could make it to the top of the rock wall, he might — just might — get himself a clear view of just what's goin' on back there.'

'Precisely,' grunted Doc. 'But as for me bein' too old — '

'Admire your spirit, Doc, but you ain't here for scalin' rock faces. I'll go. You sit it out here for an hour. If I ain't back in that time, take it as read that the passage there is worth followin'. Bring up yourself and my mount quiet as you can, and I'll join you some place.'

'And if you don't?' asked Doc.

'If I don't, you're on your own,' said the sheriff, slipping from the saddle and handing the reins to Doc. 'Let's stay lucky, eh?'

★ ★ ★

The climb along the narrow track from the floor of the pass to the jagged outline of the summit, was a deal tougher than Sheriff Grove had reckoned on.

He made fast progress through the early stages, foot and hand holds coming easily and regularly. But at the halfway stage he began to slow. His limbs were aching, his mind spinning with the concentration, the footholds less easy to find, the areas for a safe grip harder to come by. And the light, in the suddenness of the onset of evening in the mountains, beginning to fade.

He had paused, his back to the rock wall, palms of his hands flat on the smoothness of the surface, steadied his balance, glanced quickly at Doc now no more than a blurred figure far below him, and figured his next move.

He would be moving from here on at a slower pace. The climb would become increasingly difficult as the track narrowed, threatened to crumble away in parts, steepened as it went higher and, in some places, he could already see, thin to no more than the width of a boot.

Was it worth the risks, he wondered? Too late now to turn back, but the climb to come offered no attractions and a whole bucket of sweat and strain for the effort. He grunted quietly. He was doing this for Charlie Roy, he reminded himself. Charlie would do the same by him. Sure he would. In the same spirit he had stood to his word in supporting McKee.

He grunted again, steadied his balance, looked ahead and then at where he had still to climb, and moved on.

It was another half-hour of slow, painful progress before Grove paused again to take stock and catch his breath. So far, good enough, he reckoned. And without the sounds of anything, or anyone, he could not understand. If Darringo did have men positioned to guard an encampment, they were not figuring for an intrusion from this direction. But once he reached the top . . .

Had Doc made for the passage yet, he pondered, or would he wait? Had there been any sight of the marshal? And just what had happened to Charlie and his party?

He climbed again, this time with renewed purpose. He had to make it to the top before the light finally faded, to be in time to make that rendezvous with Doc, and not least before he tried reaching for the next foothold in pitch dark. He might miss.

Twenty minutes later he was on the last stretch, taking a careful balance for the final foothold, finding a grip for his bruised fingers, licking at a trickle of sweat, blinking for a clearer vision, then, like some hump-backed beast, hoisting himself from the track to the flatter rock of a new surface and, for some breathless moments, simply sprawling there exhausted.

★   ★   ★

He was a long time listening, not daring to move, conscious of the movement somewhere in the gloom to his left, a movement that could only have been made by another human. And not, he would wager, a friendly one.

He breathed slowly, silently, his eyes working frantically through a limited line of vision. The man was moving again, pacing carefully, in no hurry, measured steps, going away, turning, coming back.

One of Darringo's men? A look-out keeping watch on the pass? Had to be. But only one, he wondered, or would he have a companion close by?

Grove continued to wait, thinking now of how far Doc might have come in his progress from the pass and along the passage. What seemed a certainty was that he would eventually be seen by the routinely patrolling look-out. Doc would stand no chance. A single shot from high above him, and he would be down, dead in a matter of seconds.

The sheriff waited for the steps to turn again and move away. Now was his opportunity, he thought, coming quickly to his knees and then to two feet, crouching, watching, listening. The look-out was still pacing, moving on, his back to Grove as he prowled forward now, his Colt in one hand, the other clenched to a fist should he need it.

How far would the guard go before he turned? Could Grove risk a lunge now while the man's back was still a shape he could clearly define? He had to take the risk.

He came on in a rush, the Colt raised for the blow that would crash across the back of the look-out's head. Three strides, four, into a fifth . . . The guard went down with barely more than a gurgled grunt and lay perfectly still at Grove's feet.

He collected the *bandido*'s rifle, the knife in his belt, and scuttled low and fast to the edge of the rocks looking down on the passage. At first there was nothing in the thickening gloom, then the merest scuff of a hoof through dirt, another, soon to be a shape. A rider: Doc Whipple.

Grove signalled his presence then turned his gaze to what he could make out of the darkened canyon to his right where the glow from a freshly fuelled fire began to spread across the deepening evening sky.

They had reached Darringo's camp, but in what state would they find Charlie Roy and McKee — if they found them at all?

18

'They're goin' to kill him just for the sheer hell of it,' groaned Charlie, from the edge of the mouth of the cave. He narrowed his tired gaze on the shapes in the scene beyond the fire's glow where Raps Malone had been roped hand and foot to an upright post hammered deep into the ground. 'He ain't no more than human target practice, poor devil.' Charlie gulped on a swallow and turned to the man Darringo had ordered be brought to the cave. 'I didn't rate the fella none, but damned if I'd wish that on him. You goin' to stand by and let this happen, f'chris'sake?'

Edgar Rosen stared wide-eyed and unblinking into the gathering gloom, his face ashen and haggard as if a great age had crept up to sit on his shoulders. 'What could I possibly do?' he croaked, in a voice that sounded like dried timber cracking.

'Seems to me like you've got one helluva vested interest here, mister,' snapped Charlie. 'Ask that son of yours,' he added cynically. 'He seems to be Darringo's long-lost buddy.'

Rosen blinked but continued to stare ahead. 'I ain't unaware of my son's position, Mr Roy.'

'You bet! Care to explain just what is goin' on? Me and Mr McKee here are gettin' kinda tired of bein' shoved around in the dark — not to mention havin' our lives tossed around like trash.'

A shudder seemed to pass through Rosen's shoulders. 'Don't ask, Mr Roy. I don't think you want to know.'

'Oh, is that a fact!' flared Charlie. 'Well, pardon me for breathin', Mr-High-and-Mighty Rosen, but me and McKee have been stickin' our necks out here on your behalf, and that two-bits rag of a son of yours, and so far in this goddamn mess — '

'Stayin' alive and gettin' out of here,

is all that matters now,' clipped Rosen, a flush of colour returning to his cheeks.

'Well, I'm sure we're all relieved to hear that!' sneered Charlie, his eyes flashing. 'It's just darned decent of you to get to recognizin' it!'

McKee stepped from the shadows and laid a hand on Charlie's arm. 'Look,' he said, nodding to the figures emerging from a cave on the far side of the bowl. 'That's the other fella they've captured. Who is he?'

'A marshal,' said Rosen flatly. 'One by the name of Keetch, so my son tells me. He's been trailin' Johnny since a place called Pinecuts.'

'They goin' to rope him or just add him to the audience?' said Charlie, tightening his gaze on the figures.

'They're only watchin' for now,' said McKee. 'It's Malone who's goin' to serve as the example of what's to come.'

Charlie spat defiantly. 'That son of yours goin' to stand by and let you get served up as crow meat?' he asked, his stare on Rosen. 'You figure for that, or ain't he got no real say where Darringo's concerned?'

Sweat beaded on the rancher's face, but he stayed silent.

'Well, I guess it ain't goin' to be of no bother to me, anyhow,' shrugged Charlie, digging deep into a pocket for his pipe. 'Like you say, gettin' out of here alive — '

McKee gestured hurriedly as a heavily armed guard sauntered towards the cave.

Charlie slid to McKee's side. 'What? You seen somethin'?'

'Out there, at the passage from the pass. Somebody movin' about.'

'One of Darringo's look-outs?'

'Mebbe, but I'd swear a pan of beans to best beef that was Sheriff Grove out there.'

'Sheriff Grove?' frowned Charlie. 'Hell, if you're right that could only mean — '

Darringo's voice rang out across the night. 'And now, my friends, I, Juan

Darringo, will show you how it is when you invade his territory without an invitation.'

He raised a hand to the figures behind him. A dusky dark-haired girl twirled into the fire's glow, the layers of her skirts swirling high above her naked thighs as she danced round the roped body of Malone, a knife gleaming and flashing in her hand, her body swaying and contorting to the *bandidos*' rhythmic clapping.

'What in the name of — ?' mouthed Charlie.

The girl continued to dance provocatively, her eyes as round as winter moons, her flesh glistening with sweat, black hair lifting and falling about her neck and breasts like the surge of high tide to a shore. The clapping increased. Voices shouted, rose to a crescendo of sound as the dancer finally lunged the knife at Malone, ripping open his shirt and cutting a wound across his chest.

The blood flowed freely. The dancer disappeared in a final swirl of skirts to the shadows. A second girl took her place in the glow, this time with a spear held high above her head as she swirled to the renewed clapping and shouting.

Malone's glazed expression of fear and bewilderment seemed frozen on his sweat-soaked face. The blood still flowed, the dancer swirled, the spear-head glinted, the throng of *bandidos* closed in as if to witness the kill.

A shot rang out from Darringo's rifle as the bandit leader strode into the full glow of the crackling fire, Johnny Rosen, twin Colts holstered at his waist, a step behind.

'Wait,' the leader shouted, behind another shot high into the night sky, his grin flashing on his gleaming teeth. He raised both arms to the throng. 'Our guest here, Señor Johnny Rosen, will have the pleasure of finishing the invader.'

The crowd shouted. The dancer thrust the spear to the ground. Rosen drew the twin Colts.

Darringo lowered his arms, his gaze

tight and mean on the gunman's face, the grin drifting to a sneer. 'In your own time, *señor*, as you see fit. The prisoner is yours.'

Edgar Rosen groaned. Charlie Roy swallowed, his gaze riveted on the scene below him. McKee had already faded back to the deeper shadows, unseen, unnoticed and now unmoving, only his eyes alive to what was happening.

Johnny Rosen's guns blazed with a suddenness and finality that roared across the night as if splitting it apart. The throng cheered. Malone slumped at the stake, wide-eyed, open-mouthed, his blood coursing to the dirt at his feet.

Darringo's rifle cracked again. He gestured to the figures behind him. Seconds later Marshal Keetch was dragged into the fire glow.

Darringo called for silence. 'Señor Rosen is fearless, eh?' he smiled. 'A true *bandido*! We welcome him.' The throng cheered. Darringo slapped Rosen's back before continuing, 'And now, my compatriots, we shall have a special occasion. A real man of the law for our pleasure. A marshal no less!'

Keetch was pushed closer to the fire.

'This unfortunate, misguided gringo,' Darringo went on, 'has been stalking our good friend Señor Rosen with the sole intent of taking him to the gallows. Well, his luck has run out with Darringo, eh?'

More cheering and shouting. A rifle cracked. Men whooped. The dancers swirled their skirts in the increasing frenzy of excitement and anticipation.

'Remove the dead body,' ordered Darringo, 'and rope the marshal, then, when we have sampled our wines and victuals we shall have more pleasure! What do you say, Señor Rosen, will your guns blaze again for us? Will you take your revenge here, tonight, bury the ghost that has haunted your trail?' His vast gut rolled with his laughter. 'I think so, eh? Yes, I think so. Only this time, *señor*, take your time, make it a little slower!'

Darringo released a volley of shots to

the night. The *bandidos* shouted. The dancers swirled into action.

Johnny Rosen, the cut of his tailored shirt and pants, the high polish on his boots still a mark of his standing in spite of the dirt of the bandit's lair, stared hard at the man being roped. There was no doubting that he would do precisely as Darringo ordered when the time came.

And Marshal Keetch, wincing as the ropes tightened, knew it.

* * *

Charlie Roy stiffened, his gaze flat, wet and dismayed in the lifting glow of the huge camp-fire where the *bandidos*, the *señoritas*, dancers and followers were gathered now to sup their wines and sample the platters of food being handed round.

Darringo and Johnny Rosen stood apart, deep in conversation and doubtless, thought Charlie, plotting their future exploits. The roped marshal

171

simply stared ahead.

Edgar Rosen had turned his back on the glow, the gathering, the sounds and walked to the rear of the cave like a man in a trance. The look in his eyes seemed to have resigned him to a nightmare.

But McKee still had his gaze concentrated on the blurred, shadowy mouth of the passage. And it was he, minutes later, who came silently to Charlie's side to whisper, 'I think I see a chance.'

19

'Hell,' hissed Doc Whipple, easing his aching body to a new position in the rocks, 'have you ever seen anythin' like that?'

Sheriff Grove shifted his feet and flicked his gaze anxiously over the shadows. 'Not my side of Red Creeks I ain't, and that's a fact.' He eased back to check on the mounts at the mouth of the passage, glanced quickly again over the sheer rock walls, and slid back to Doc's side. 'Might start gettin' a mite dangerous round here. We should move before them rats miss the look-out they posted.'

'And where we movin' to, you figured that?' asked Doc. 'Soon as them *bandidos* have supped enough, they're goin' to get to whoopin' it up again, not to mention makin' one almighty mess of the marshal out there. I wouldn't give a spit for his chances right now.'

Grove swallowed and tightened his gaze. 'We've got to try makin' contact with Charlie and McKee.' He frowned suddenly and deeply. 'And here's another thought for you, Doc, who in tarnation is the fella in the fancy cut and polished boots who did for Malone with them blazin' Colts? Where the hell did he spring from?'

'You tell me,' said Doc, 'but I'll drop this thought with you before we make a move: minute I clapped eyes on that slick dude, I had one almighty alarmin' notion — he sure as hell has the looks and bearin' of Edgar Rosen.'

Grove stared into Doc's eyes. 'You mean — '

'I ain't sayin' for no certain fact, but supposin' the body McKee discovered out at Long Ridge weren't that of Johnny Rosen, but supposin' that silver chain had at some time belonged to him and been deliberately placed in the rocks to convince whoever found the dead man that Johnny Rosen had been shot and robbed by *bandidos*. Now that would be one helluva way of gettin' a trailin' marshal off your back if you happened to be on the run. You get my thinkin', Sheriff?'

'You bet,' said Grove, blinking as he began to sweat. 'Yeah . . . ' he added thoughtfully, rubbing his chin. 'But right now, Doc, that don't help us none, but here's somethin' that might. Supposin' we hitch these mounts safe and try makin' our way round the main camp towards them caves on the far side there. If Darringo's goin' to be holdin' Charlie and McKee anywhere, it'll be there. What do you reckon?'

'Got to do somethin',' agreed Doc. 'Can't just stand by while Darringo goes about killin' at will, though what we're goin' to be able to do for the marshal beats me.'

Grove grunted. 'Me too. But like you say, waitin' ain't gettin' us nowhere. Let's go . . . '

★ ★ ★

'How?' hissed Charlie. 'How we goin' to do it with all them guns and God only knows what else ranged against us? Hell, that's some tall order, mister.' Charlie's eyes flicked from McKee to the guard lounging on the far side of the mouth of the cave, his rifle sloped casually in his arms, a newly opened bottle of hootch at his feet.

'Get rid of him to start with,' whispered McKee. 'Give it just long enough for him to get a good sampling of that bottle, then leave him to me.'

'You ain't armed, f'chris'sake.'

'Don't you believe it, Mr Roy. I'm standin' on a knife — a blade in the false sole of my right boot.' A soft smile flickered at McKee's lips. 'They always overlook a fella's feet!'

'Mebbe,' persisted Charlie, 'but I still don't see how — '

'I'm pretty certain that's Sheriff Grove out there,' said McKee. 'Could be there's others with him. If we can join up there's mebbe goin' to be a way of savin' that marshal. But first things first. Let's put Rosen in the picture. We're goin' to need his help.'

Charlie peered towards the back of the cave where Rosen stood alone. 'He don't look to be of use to anybody right now. Full of remorse, regrets and who knows what else? I ain't sure he's goin' to be worth trustin'.'

'Well, we can't leave him. Let's try.'

It was Charlie who finally managed to get to the rancher's side and fix his concentration on what McKee was planning.

'You with us, Mr Rosen?' asked Charlie.

'I'm with you, Mr Roy. It's the only thing we can do. We must make the effort.'

'What about your son?'

Rosen was silent for a moment. 'What about him?' he said. 'He seems to have made his own choices. He's no son of mine.'

'That's easy to say, Mr Rosen, and I reckon I know how you must feel, but when it comes to it blood is a whole sight thicker than water.'

Rosen fixed a flat, expressionless stare on Charlie's face. 'Let's get movin', shall we?'

★ ★ ★

But it was to be close on another half-hour before Charlie, McKee and Edgar Rosen were finally able to make their first move.

The *bandidos* at the fire were still drinking, eating, whooping and shouting, their mood now one of fevered frenzy as the girls danced, the flames leapt, the shadows loomed and faded like giant birds in flight, and the night air grew steadily thicker and hotter in the excitement.

Marshal Keetch had done his best to do what he could to help himself, his flexing fingers and writhing wrists working tirelessly against the rope binding them. But the progress to loosen the tightness was slow and painful, and he knew with every minute that passed that he was probably struggling against the inevitable: Darringo's dancers would taunt him until the time came for Johnny Rosen to make the kill.

But when that moment came, Keetch resolved, he would make sure that the young gunslinger lived out the rest of his days with the memory of the look in a dying man's eyes that would haunt him forever.

The *bandido* guarding the mouth of the cave had worked diligently at the bottle of hootch, the taste and pleasure of it increasing with every mouthful. McKee waited until he judged the man's senses and reactions sufficiently dulled before he finally knelt on one knee seemingly to adjust the fit of his right boot. When he stood fully upright again he glanced quickly at Charlie and Rosen, nodded and sauntered casually towards the guard.

Charlie saw nothing of the fatal thrust, heard nothing of the man's groan as McKee eased the suddenly dead body to a sitting position with its back to a boulder in full view of the throng at the fire, wiped the knife-blade clean, slid it to his belt and gestured for Charlie and Rosen to join him.

They moved swiftly but silently from the cave to the deepest shadows, threading their way like insects from rock to rock, boulder to boulder on a path towards the entrance to the passage. Twice they were forced to sink flat on their stomachs at the approach of patrolling guards; twice they lay prone, praying, listening, waiting for McKee to signal to move on. Twice they survived.

Charlie reckoned they had been moving some twenty minutes when McKee's urgent indication to drop low raised the sweat in his neck.

What now, he wondered, another guard? They had been halted some five minutes before the signal came to move to the left to where it seemed the deepest depths of the night lay in waiting. Once into the darkness, with their eyesight adjusting to determine shapes, Charlie became aware of the familiar figure of Doc Whipple at McKee's side, then a second, the unmistakable bulk of Sheriff Grove.

He heaved a sigh of relief at the whispered tones of Doc's voice. 'God-damnit, you could've gotten yourself killed creepin' about like that! Good to see you.'

The five men huddled together in the rocks, quickly exchanging accounts of what had happened since leaving Red Creeks.

'Hell,' hissed Charlie at last. 'We've sure got one almighty mess on our hands here. What's the priority?'

'That's got to be the marshal out there,' murmured Grove. 'He's mebbe countin' down the minutes he's got left even now.'

'Any suggestions?' asked Doc, his eyes flashing in the darkness.

'A diversion,' said McKee. 'Some-thin' big enough to worry even Darringo. His horses. He ain't goin' nowhere in this country without horses. So we scatter that hitched line back there. And fast by the sound of it.'

The huddled group fell silent against the rising crescendo of shouts and whoops as the dancers swirled again and the flames of the fire leapt to the night like the tongues of Hell itself.

20

McKee lowered his arm in his crouching position, put a finger to his lips for absolute silence, and nodded to the figure three yards to the back of him. Sheriff Grove acknowledged with the faintest lift of his hand, and waited.

The men had left the rocks on the decision by McKee that any attempt to release the horses on the hitch line was essentially a job for no more than two. 'Too many hands and we might foul up,' he had whispered. 'I'm suggestin' myself and the sheriff here. The rest of you stay low and silent.'

Charlie had been conscious of a suddenly lost, grey, empty look in Edgar Rosen's eyes, as if, in the seething mess of his thoughts, he had cause to wonder: push on, get out, where to? And had only the echoes of his own doubts in answer.

McKee indicated for Grove to move to within earshot. 'We're close,' he whispered. 'I figure for only two guards, one at the far end, one patrollin'. I'll take the patrol.' He drew the knife from his belt. 'On my signal, you take the second. Use your Colt, but no shootin'. Then we release the horses, scatter them, and head for the passage to the pass. Doc, Charlie and Rosen will meet us there.'

'And then?' hissed the sheriff.

'That's the future,' said McKee, balancing the knife in his grip. 'We ain't there yet.'

★   ★   ★

All that might have been seen of McKee in those next minutes was the shadowy drift of his shape as he moved among the rocks at the hitch line. The mounts were already a touch nervy in the constant lift and fall of the shouts and yells, the sudden whoops to the dancers' swirls and provocative taunts,

184

the leaping flames of the refuelled fire, the flying sparks and surging columns and tides of shadows that charged from the glow like an army.

McKee murmured softly to the horses, his steps slow but measured and precise. No stumbles, no scrapes. He glanced back once to assure himself that Sheriff Grove had moved, then slid on searching now for the patrolling guard.

It was another half-minute before he had the slimly built *bandido* in his sights; an easy moving but reluctant look-out who would much sooner have been relishing the dancing *señoritas* than walking a line of restless mounts. Fate had drawn him a very short straw this night, but maybe Darringo would not forget him or his companion. They would have their rewards later.

The *bandido* had paused once again to listen to the shouts and yells of the now drink-soaked voices, the whooping encouragement for the *señoritas* to dance faster, reveal more flesh. The guard spat his disappointment, cradled his rifle across his chest and moved on, grumbling quietly at the back of his throat. Their world was a cruel place . . .

He had reached a thicker, heavier sprawl of rocks and boulders when he halted again, this time with the rifle slipping easily to his firm hold on the barrel and stock. He had heard a noise, or perhaps seen a shape. Or perhaps the long night, the spooked horses, the pleasures beyond his reach were getting to him. Perhaps he should see somebody about being relieved. Damn it, he had been here —

But his thoughts had gone no further. He had opened his mouth to shout at the first surge of fiery pain in his back, but there had been no voice, no sounds from a mouth that opened but was dry and silent, and then only an agonizing inability to move or call out as the pain increased like a spreading fire before a total darkness descended.

McKee eased the dead body to the ground, cleaned the knife and removed the *bandido*'s own blade from the sheath on his belt. He peered ahead for Grove's signal, waited, the shouts of the frenzied throng ringing in his ears. Should he cut the line now, continue to wait, move to help the sheriff? He gritted his teeth, seethed through a tightening breath — and then saw the wave.

He had slashed the line and was scattering the snorting, whinnying, wild-eyed mounts when Grove stumbled, sweating and breathless to his side.

'Line's down at that end. Horses are free,' he gasped. 'You ready?'

'Ready,' grunted McKee. 'Let's shift, head for the passage, before all hell breaks loose.'

★   ★   ★

It broke loose in a volley of rifle fire, the suddenly angered shouts and bellows of the *bandidos*, screams from the dancers, and the yelling of Darringo.

'Round up the horses! Bring the prisoners to me! Search everywhere. Cut that marshal free and take him to the caves . . .'

'Hear that?' murmured Doc from the shadows. 'Marshal's goin' to be free. Mebbe we can get to him now. We goin' to try?'

'Wait,' said McKee, glancing at the others where they huddled in the cover of boulders at the mouth to the passage. 'Let's see where they take him. Blunderin' about blind in the dark could blunt the edge we've just won. Give it ten minutes.'

'Meantime,' murmured Doc again, 'we've got another problem.' He waited for the tone of his voice to sink in. 'Tell them, Charlie.'

'We've lost our horses,' said the scout flatly, tapping the bowl of his empty pipe in the palm of his hand. 'The mounts Doc left here in the pass bolted in the mayhem, and them we were ridin' when Darringo took us prisoner were hitched on the line in the camp.

So we're horseless. All we've got is our legs and feet, and one helluva lot of climbin' and walkin' to do if we're ever goin' to come out of these mountains alive.'

'Mebbe we can round up some mounts,' suggested Rosen, becoming aware for the first time of the reality of the situation.

'Mebbe,' acknowledged Charlie. 'But it's a long shot. We might get lucky and snaffle one, but any more . . . ' He shrugged. 'Like I say a long shot.'

'So what you sayin', Mr Roy?' asked McKee.

Charlie considered for a moment. 'Only a matter of minutes now before Darringo realizes what's happened and that we're on the run. And then he's goin' to come huntin' — and believe me he knows these mountains like the backs of his own hands.' He paused. 'But we've mebbe got just one edge, if we can use it quickly.'

'That bein'?' frowned Grove.

'If we can clear this passage, Snake

189

Pass and the far reaches of the ridge, we can push on to pass round Cloud Peak and head for Rock Tor.'

'The tor?' hissed Doc. 'Hell, that's a graveyard. Even Darringo would think twice about crossin' Rock Tor.'

'That's our edge,' said Charlie. 'The only real chance we've got, specially on foot.'

'Then we take it,' snapped Rosen, something of his old authority gleaming in his eyes.

'Not so fast,' urged Grove. 'What about Keetch? Can't pull out without doin' somethin' for him. Mebbe we should try — '

'No need,' clipped Doc through a tight breath. 'Somebody's headin' this way now, and my bettin' would be . . . It's him. It's the marshal.'

* * *

They waited in a tense silence for Keetch to clear the last few rocks and boulders at the mouth to the passage and stumble, breathless and sweat-soaked, into the huddle of five men. He glanced anxiously behind him, satisfied himself that *bandidos* were not hot-footing on his heels, and relaxed.

'How'd you manage that?' asked Grove.

'Brute force and a lot of luck,' gasped Keetch. 'Them scum are a whole sight more concerned about roundin'-up spooked horses than holdin' on to men.'

He glanced round the other faces watching him as Doc introduced McKee, Charlie Roy and Edgar Rosen, his eyes resting tight and fixed on the rancher.

'I've come a long way to meet you, mister,' he croaked on his dry, dusty throat.

'A long way to bring in my son, I think,' said Rosen, stiffening. 'I don't know what your chances might be from here on in.'

'I'll take them whatever they are,' grunted Keetch.

'We're wastin' valuable time here,' snapped Doc, his eyes darting like lights to the still lifting flames of the fire behind him, the shouting, yelling, bellowed orders and staccato screaming of the dancing girls. 'No time to tell you what we've got planned, Marshal,' he explained hurriedly. 'Just take it as read that the options ain't exactly in abundance; same goes for our weapons, but we've got the best mountain scout hereabouts leadin' us. Destination: Rock Tor, and don't tell us it's a graveyard. We know, but that's the only option in town against the blood-thirsty rabble back of us. Shall we go?'

21

Charlie Roy narrowed his gaze on the mist-shrouded crags of Cloud Peak, traced the tracks that led down the rock faces to the trail winding round the outcrops at the base, and tapped McKee on the arm.

'Just one,' he murmured, pointing to the lone figure climbing the southern face. 'But one's enough and one too many.'

McKee grunted. 'We could take him out. One good shot.'

'Too risky at this time of day. Shot would echo for a dozen miles. Darringo would have us pinpointed like rats in a trap. No, I figure for leavin' him. He's a lone scout, and mebbe worn through after the night's activities. He won't be hurryin'.'

McKee eased the grip of his hat. 'Warn the others and we'll push on.

How far to the tor now?'

'Half a day if we stay lucky. A lot will depend on how quickly Darringo's regrouped his main band and got them mounted. He won't shift without horses. Fella out there is just a feeler keepin' a track on where Darringo reckons we might be headin'. He'll figure for the tor, sure enough, but he'll want to hit us long before that.'

The men lay silent in the rocks for a moment, their gazes fixed on the lone figure.

'Will Johnny Rosen ride with Darringo?' murmured McKee. 'Against his own father?'

'Ain't no love lost in that family. That sonofabitch, Johnny Rosen, has got some answerin' to do, and more than one life to swing for from what the marshal tells.' Charlie pondered for a moment. 'But it's like I always say, blood is a whole sight thicker than water when it comes to it. I wouldn't wager a cent either side of what Edgar Rosen might do at a showdown, or what he's thinkin' right now. If it were me . . . But it ain't, so I guess all we can do right now is tackle what's facin' us best we can. And that, mister, is goin' to need some effort.'

Charlie eased himself out of the rock cover and turned his back on the lone lookout. 'Due east from here,' he announced. 'Let's not waste the light.'

★ ★ ★

They walked, scrambled, climbed, and sometimes stumbled, in a single file, Charlie Roy leading, Sheriff Grove bringing up the rear.

Their destination, according to Charlie, was dead ahead. 'See that white wall of mist?' he had said, pointing to the thick, swirling mass below the higher peaks. 'We're goin' to go through that, then drop rapidly to the floor of Rock Tor. You'll be seein' it soon enough for yourselves, so I'll save my breath on what you'll find.'

'But by my scant reckonin', Mr Roy,'

195

Rosen had frowned, 'we'll be headin' *away* from Red Creeks if we follow that route. Shouldn't we be headin' west?'

'Sure we should,' Charlie had grinned, sucking on his empty pipe, 'but if we did we'd be meetin' Darringo and his rats head-on. This way we draw them towards a territory not even they have a deal of stomach for.'

'And if we make it?' Rosen had pursued.

'Right now we're still only tryin'. So let's try, eh?'

They had been going a long hour and were already into the chillier outer veils of the mist, when Charlie called a halt and motioned for the line to close up.

'Don't lose sight of whoever's in front of you from here on. But don't call out neither if you get cut off. Stay right where you are and wait. We'll come and find you.' Charlie filled and lit his pipe. 'We'll be through this mist in a couple of hours at worst. Then we'll rest up. Meantime, we know there's at least one *bandido* searchin' to pick up our trail. My bettin' is there's others not too far distant, so stay alert to sounds and movements you can't readily figure.'

They moved on, but with new thoughts to occupy their minds.

Doc Whipple was contemplating the arthritis in his right knee and trying not to convince himself that it was only going to get worse from here on.

Sheriff Grove was worrying about the lack of weapons among them; the fact that they had no horses and little prospect of getting their hands on any, and the mood of Edgar Rosen who might, he thought, do anything at almost anytime.

McKee, perhaps more than any of them, listened and remained acutely aware of the possibility of the *bandidos* being a whole sight closer than Charlie had reckoned. Darringo was no fool when it came to mountain tracking, and he had the manpower to distribute a force that would scurry like ants through the rocks.

And then there was the whole gnawing question of Johnny Rosen. Had he really joined up with Darringo? Was that because he had no other place to run? What would he do in a showdown face-to-face with his pa? Just how thick was a man's family blood?

They were deep into the blanket of mist when Edgar Rosen disappeared.

★ ★ ★

It was Doc Whipple who first noticed the sudden disappearance of the figure at his side. 'He was here. Damnit, I could reach out and touch him. Right here, I tell you. So what's the darned fool thinkin' of? You told him, Charlie, told everybody straight up what to do.'

'Rosen's choice is of his own makin',' said Charlie, squinting at the blurred shapes of the others. 'We push on. No hangin' back in these conditions. If Rosen catches up, so be it. If he don't . . . '

'It'll be that son of his,' reflected

Keetch, easing his hat to scratch his head. 'He's gone in search of him again. Mebbe thinkin' he can talk him round or somethin'. Some chance! Darringo'll more likely slit his throat soon as spit on him. Darned fool.'

McKee put a finger to his lips. 'Quiet,' he whispered.

Doc Whipple felt a cold beading of sweat on his brow as the mist seemed to gather like a shroud and the silence closed in.

The men stood without a movement between them, listening for something that might be anything, anywhere, or nothing at all, no more than McKee's fancy. They waited, in one moment chilled by the mist, in the next conscious of their tension, the trickle of sweat, the faster beat of the heart.

McKee's eyes narrowed, widened. His fingers fell instinctively to the bone handle of the blade at his belt. Grove's grip on his rifle tightened. Keetch's gaze narrowed. Charlie swallowed.

'You hear somethin'?' hissed Doc,

glancing at McKee, who again motioned for silence. 'I ain't pickin' up nothin' save — '

A trickle of loose rocks somewhere deep in the mist behind them split the silence as if ripping it.

McKee's arm went out to signal no movements. Charlie's shoulders twitched nervously. Grove levelled the rifle on a target he could neither see nor hear.

'Mebbe it's Rosen,' murmured Doc.

McKee gestured again, this time for the others to crouch lower. He glanced quickly at Grove and Keetch, pointed ahead, and crept forward under the levelled aim of the sheriff's rifle barrel. He was fading to a vague, distorted blur within seconds.

They heard the slow glide of his boots over stone; could almost hear his breath as he closed on whatever he had heard and now perhaps could see. Charlie fancied he glimpsed for a moment the glint of the drawn blade. Doc would have sworn he could smell fear but whether his own or another's he was not so certain.

A second trickle of rocks, then silence, total and suffocating for what seemed minutes. Charlie wanted to move, but could barely raise an arm. Doc sweated freely and stifled a shiver at the same time, but the sheriff's grip on the rifle remained firm and steady. Keetch remained motionless. It was only a matter of time.

A scuffle, groans, a throttled scream of pain. Grove plunged forward, followed by the marshal, shots blazing from somewhere within seconds.

Charlie cursed at the suddenly spiralling echoes. 'Sons-of-goddamn-bitches, they've found us!' he spat, at the same time pulling Doc lower to the covering of scant rock.

The mist swirled, heavy now with cordite and the heat of shooting. A man yelled. Grove shouted a string of curses. Charlie lunged out of cover.

'Easy,' yelled McKee at last. 'They're dead. Three of 'em. Two knifed. One shot.' He stumbled through the mist,

Grove and Keetch at his side, clutching what they could carry of captured knives and weapons, a length of rope, a bandoleer and canteens of water.

The men gulped, swallowed, sweated, stood in silence for a while before Charlie's voice cut across the still thin, chilled air.

'They're movin' a whole sight faster than I'd figured for,' he reflected quietly. 'And now they're goin' to know exactly where we are.'

'Damn it, we had no choice,' said Doc. 'It was them or us.'

'How far behind do you figure Darringo for bein'?' asked McKee, stoppering a stolen canteen. 'Can't be more than a mile or so.'

'He's trailed overnight,' murmured Charlie, his gaze narrowing as if to strip aside the veils of mist. 'Them's foot soldiers he put out — and there'll be more. Dozens of the rats.'

'So push on fast for the tor, eh?' said Grove. 'Nowhere else to go.'

Charlie grunted and pondered for a

moment. 'No sign of Rosen,' he reflected again, 'which probably means he's continued down to the lower reaches. Darringo will be plannin' on makin' it there by full sun-up, so mebbe we've won ourselves some time.' He scratched his chin. 'But we ain't goin' down. Nossir. Prepare yourselves for a climb — and, believe me, I mean climb.'

22

'He handled that knife like it'd been grafted to his hand,' murmured Sheriff Grove at Charlie's side as the two men led the group working its way through the mist-shrouded plateau. 'Fast as light. Them *bandidos* never saw a thing. I tell you straight, Charlie, that fella McKee makes his own law when it comes to survival — blade law.' He grunted quietly as he reached for the next safe foothold. 'Give a year's salary for a half-dozen like him right now.'

'No chance of that,' said Charlie, slowing the pace a moment to assess their position. He squinted against the swirling mist. 'Just be grateful he's on our side.'

Doc Whipple gulped and was grateful for McKee's helping hand as the pair followed in Charlie's wake. 'Tell you somethin' for nothin', mister, if I come out of this in one piece — '

'You will,' said McKee, strengthening his grip on Doc's arm. 'We all will.'

'I ain't so sure about Rosen,' said Doc. 'That son of his don't deserve to, but as for Rosen himself, hell, that's something else. Wouldn't give much for his chances.' He waited for Keetch to catch up through the mist. 'What do you reckon, Marshal? You got any notion on Rosen's thinkin'?'

'Could be he's still harbourin' some hope of talkin' sense into Johnny's head,' said Keetch. 'But I fancy that for bein' no better than spittin' on the wind. Darringo, on the other hand, will be thinkin' extortion, if he can make it work and somehow get his hands on the Montana fortune. He'll be dealin' for the whole pot make no mistake.'

'You goin' to get your man?' asked Doc bluntly. 'Heck, you've been trailin' him for long enough.'

The marshal lapsed to a thoughtful silence, his gaze flat on the swirls and shrouding mist where there was never more than a blur of shapes. 'Somebody's goin' to get him,' was all he said, hitching the coiled rope at his shoulder and taking a firmer, one-handed grip on his rifle.

The line of men continued to move on, threading their slow way across the plateau of strewn rocks and boulders, Charlie pausing from time to time to almost sniff out the way ahead, his every scouting instinct alive and alerted, his mind working frantically through memory.

There had been no further sight or sounds of Darringo's men, even though the group knew well enough and could feel they were out there somewhere, waiting shapes behind the mist.

They had been going another hour when Charlie raised an arm for a halt and pointed ahead to the grey wall of jagged crags, fissures, perilous ledges and footholds across sheer rock faces.

'And now we climb,' he announced.

★   ★   ★

No one had questioned McKee's assumed leadership when it came to the actual physical effort. Charlie had pointed the way to where they wanted to be by the time the sun had finally burned off the low cloud and mist, and McKee had set about making sure they would be there by the safest, if not the fastest, route possible.

'Hadn't figured him for a mountain man,' the marshal had noted quietly to Sheriff Grove.

'Hadn't figured him for a lot of things,' the lawman had quipped. 'But I ain't fussin' over the surprises! Seems to know what he's doin', and that's all that matters.'

Even so, and much as Keetch and Grove were grateful to leave the climbing to McKee's orders, neither man had closed his mind to what might be lurking behind the next twist of rock, the clammy mist. 'Keep your eyes skinned real good,' Charlie had urged. 'Darringo won't be reckonin' on us takin' this route to the tor, but he'll figure it soon enough. And somewhere hereabouts he's goin' to be waitin'.'

Doc Whipple had done the best he could not to delay the others once the climb got underway, but age and worn limbs were a burden, and Doc, like it or not, struggled and suffered.

He came quickly to McKee's attention. 'At your pace, Doc,' he had murmured, looking back at Doc's progress. 'We ain't for leavin' nobody, and not for losin' none either, so take your time.'

'That's all very well,' Doc had wheezed, 'but I ain't no young fella any more, nor is Charlie there. All this takes a bit of doin' at our age. Tell you somethin' else — '

But Doc's words had been lost in the sudden crack of rifle shots and his voice buried in the eerie whine of the echoes that followed.

'Hell,' cursed Charlie, clinging to the rocks like a lizard.

Doc gulped and groaned. Sheriff Grove tried to half turn to look back to the plateau they had just crossed and almost lost his footing.

'They've got us pinned here, damn it,' called Keetch. 'They'll pick us off like flies.'

'Climb!' ordered McKee. 'Make for the ledge to the right. There's rock cover and a small cave. Shift!'

The men climbed, Keetch reaching to help Doc, the sheriff looking to where Charlie was fighting to find the next handhold.

McKee had climbed on ahead at a rapid pace to reach the ledge, check it out for their safety then turn to lend a hand to the others as one by one they slid, scrambled, slithered to the scant cover of the rocks and collapsed, breathless, shaken and sweating.

Keetch was the last to reach the ledge. 'No more shots, so what was that — a warning?'

'You've got it,' said McKee, his gaze working frantically over the wall of mist. 'Darringo seems to have got ahead of us again. The plan'll be to keep us pinned down here 'til the main body of men arrives.'

'It's vital we keep movin',' said Charlie. 'We can't afford to stop.' His old eyes gleamed. 'If we're still on this ledge in an hour, we're here for keeps.'

★　★　★

The mist cleared rapidly, the sun burned through the cloud like a disc of flame, and the flies began to buzz and pester.

'Any sign of the rats?' asked Doc, crawling to McKee's side in the rock cover. 'Charlie's still frettin'. Says we've just got to get higher. But the way I see it, if we move out now, they'll simply start shootin' — and you can't climb and shoot back at the same time.'

'So we fight from here,' said McKee.

'Oh, sure,' nodded Doc. 'How and with what? We'd be wastin' lead just pepperin' the rocks down there in the hope of hittin' one of the rats.'

'No shootin'. Like you say a waste of

lead.' McKee motioned for the others to move closer. 'We're goin' to have to work in two groups. Charlie, you're goin' to lead Doc and the sheriff here to the higher reaches. You're the only one who knows where we're goin', so you lead.'

'And you?' asked Grove.

'Me and the marshal are goin' to do our best to create a diversion,' smiled McKee. 'I don't figure for there bein' more than two or three scumbags down there. They need somethin' to occupy 'em, so we're goin' to pepper the rats with rocks. There's enough loose boulders here to give 'em quite a scare. I've checked. And while they're dealin' with rocks, you, Charlie, will be climbin'.'

'Will it work?' frowned Doc.

'It's goin' to have to,' said Keetch.

'Get yourselves ready,' murmured McKee, slipping away to the clutter of rocks and stones. 'You move on my command.' He motioned to the marshal. 'Help yourself,' he grinned, 'and stay on target!'

★ ★ ★

The onslaught on the hidden *bandidos* began with a hail of smaller rocks hurled blind by McKee and Keetch in an attempt to locate their exact position and lure them into returning fire.

The first shots cracked across the morning in less than a minute. 'One, two, three,' counted Keetch. 'You were right: there's three of them down there.'

'Keep throwin',' urged McKee. 'We'll give 'em the bigger ones once Charlie and the others are movin'.'

The bombardment continued without easing until the sweat was dripping from the two men and the supply of rocks that could be handled quickly began to dwindle.

'See that boulder to my left?' croaked McKee, hurling another rock, 'I'm goin' to try shiftin' it. Mebbe set up some sort of landslide. I'll call for your help when I'm ready.'

'How's Charlie doin'?'

'Climbin'. Another ten minutes or

so and he'll be leadin' Doc and the sheriff round that overhang and out of gunshot range. Keep your fingers crossed.'

The volley of shots grew increasingly spasmodic and aimed more in frustration than with any real judgement. Maybe the *bandidos* were running out of ammunition; maybe their target was becoming more elusive. Whatever, thought Keetch, scrambling for the rocks he could reach with his grazed and bleeding fingers, the climbers were buying valuable time, gaining distance, and would soon have a firm foothold on the notorious wilderness known as Rock Tor.

McKee heaved, hissed, spat, tensed his back muscles again and for the first time felt the boulder begin to move.

He took a deep breath, settled his hands flat on the rock surface, closed his eyes briefly for a moment, then summoned every ounce of strength within him for another heave.

The boulder groaned at its base.

Keetch turned his attention from the smaller rocks to McKee's efforts. 'Hold on,' he croaked, lending his own weight to the effort. The boulder creaked and groaned again. Small chippings broke clear as the bulk finally gave up its roots to the heaving men.

It left the ledge with a suddenness and momentum that almost carried McKee with it. 'Get to the next one, fast,' he wheezed, disregarding the loosened boulder as he crawled to the side of another bulk.

Keetch paused just long enough to see the weight crash and splinter then shower the lower rocks with a hail of chippings behind the roaring echo of a shattering boom.

Three more boulders had gone the way of the first when McKee finally lay back, exhausted and gasping. 'See anythin'?' he gulped, struggling to support himself on one elbow.

'You bet,' murmured Keetch, peering at the scene far below him. 'You'd reckon an avalanche had hit the place.

But that ain't the important thing. Know what, my friend, there ain't nothin' movin' down there no more — and the silence is golden!'

McKee lay back again and smiled.

23

Charlie set a fast pace to the wilderness of Rock Tor, where, even though the sun was high and the heat thickening, there was a chill which seeped through to a man's bones.

'Feel that?' said Doc, pulling at the collar of his shirt as if to hug himself against a draught. 'That is the breath of ghosts by my reckonin'.'

Sheriff Grove grunted. Marshal Keetch narrowed his gaze on the sprawl of grey rock-strewn land ahead and offered no comment. None was necessary. Doc Whipple was probably right.

McKee winced quietly at the still throbbing ache in his shoulders. They had successfully stalled Darringo's scouting guns, but what lay ahead? Would the *bandido* leader take his men across the tor? Would his men with their superstitions and deep-rooted beliefs, dare to follow?

Charlie called a halt and squatted in the cover of boulders. 'We're doin' well,' he murmured, his expression tense, his eyes alert for all the tiredness behind them. 'Specially now we've got them guns off our backs.' He nodded to McKee and Keetch. 'But there's still one helluva lot to do.'

'You worked it through yet?' asked Grove.

Charlie pondered quietly for a moment. 'If memory serves me well — twenty years or more back — there's an old mountain-lion track on the western side of the tor. T'ain't much, and it sure as sun-up ain't easy goin', but *if* it's as I recall, we can edge our ways down to the plains land beyond. And once there . . . Yeah, well, one thing at a time, eh? Let's get clear of this hell-hole.'

'Will Darringo know of this track?' ventured Keetch.

'Mebbe not,' said Charlie. 'A mite

before his time up here when I found it.'

Doc grunted. 'Trouble is he's got enough men to find anythin' once he gets started.' He grunted again. 'And what about the Rosens? What do you figure's happened to them, if anythin? Mebbe they're just stayin' along of Darringo.'

'They'd best just do that if they want to stay alive,' quipped Keetch. 'They ain't goin' no place.'

'But we are,' announced Charlie, standing upright. 'Two hours of steady goin', that's all we need. So let's push our luck again, shall we?'

★   ★   ★

Sheriff Grove reckoned they had been trekking close on an hour when they heard the shouts — the voices of Darringo's men lifting and echoing far below and ahead of them.

Keetch halted; Charlie gestured to keep low; Doc Whipple took a moment to mop his dirt and sweat-stained face. McKee, bringing up the rear, listened carefully, trying hard to pinpoint the calls.

'They've come round by the old trappers' route,' hissed Charlie. 'A short-cut from the ridge.' He concentrated his listening. 'They're close. Some place below to the west.'

The shouting continued, pausing only when the clatter of hoofs on rocks warned that the band was on the move, sometimes circling to the left, sometimes to the right.

'Darringo's splittin' his forces,' said Keetch, his concentration etched deep on his face.

'Surroundin' the tor,' murmured Grove.

'So what's the plan now?' frowned Doc.

Charlie drummed his fingers on the surface of a boulder, his gaze moving slowly over the grey haunted scene. The ghosts of the long dead might drift across it at any time, he thought, on a low grunt to himself. 'Best push on, but we need to know Darringo's strength and just where he's positionin' his men.'

'My job,' said Keetch, already adjusting the set of his hat, hitching his pants then freshening his grip on his Winchester. 'You keep goin'. I'll catch up later.'

Charlie nodded, the group moved on, and Keetch faded into the grey light.

★ ★ ★

The marshal reached the edge of the tor to his right and eased into the cover of a cluster of jagged rocks. The slopes and mounds below were bathed in the rich glare of sunlight, the shadows deep and heavy. Boulders stood like guards; scrub lay skeletal and twisted, the dust and dirt a shimmering skein.

He blinked, squeezed forward for a clearer view and had spotted the figure weaving his way like an ant through the rocks, when a movement at his back and the click of a primed gun hammer froze him where he crouched.

'Hold your breath, mister, and ease that rifle to the dirt real slow.' The voice was young, but firm and assured, with something of a sneer of contempt behind its confidence. Johnny Rosen, Keetch decided, was not for being messed with.

'Been a long time, Johnny,' said the marshal, turning as he eased the Winchester to the ground. 'Began to wonder if I'd ever see this day.'

Rosen's tight expression relaxed on a smooth grin. 'Make the most of it, Marshal, 'cus you sure as hell ain't long for this earth. I ain't got the time for you, and neither had Darringo, so let's get to the cut of this and be done.'

'You're holdin' the full deck, mister, the dealin's all yours. But before you get to addin' to your tally of dead men — and women — why Darringo, how'd you figure on teamin' up with him and his bunch of cut-throats? Goin' to spend best part of your days lookin' to your back in their company. They'll shoot you as soon as spit.'

Rosen's grin relaxed. 'Since you're askin', lawman, I'll tell you. I'd heard of Darringo long back. He's my kind: goes his own way, stays his own man in his own country to his own set of laws. No feather-beddin', cowpunchin' life for him.' He paused. The grin spread again. 'So, after Pinecuts, I and my colleagues opted for Darringo and the mountains. Simple as that.'

'The body McKee found bein' one of your so-called 'Colleagues'? The silver chain left purposely?'

'Correct,' sneered Rosen. 'Such men are dispensable, but served as a neat deception, 'ceptin' I didn't reckon on my fool pa saddlin' up in search of me and meetin' up with McKee. That was unfortunate, but not beyond bein' resolved.'

'And now I suppose you'll put your father to good use, drain him of his money fast as you can and — '

The Colt in Rosen's grip probed

forward. 'Enough,' he snapped. 'I'm wastin' good time, and there's the rest of your miserable bunch to take care of yet.'

'How'd you get up here so fast?' said Keetch, stalling now for all the time he could win, his eyes flitting quickly from Rosen to the rocks, to the shadows and shapes around him.

'Don't underrate Darringo, mister. He can read these mountains and tell you how men are goin' to react to them better than a hawk.' The Colt probed again. 'And now — '

Keetch kicked out wildly at the rocks nearest his right boot. The Colt blazed, the shot skimming the marshal's shoulder to singe the cloth of his shirt. Rosen growled, fired again. Keetch fell back under the momentum of his own flaying arms and legs.

'Sonofabitch,' cursed Rosen, levelling for a third shot.

Keetch launched himself to the cover of a larger boulder, certain now that it would not be the crunch of his bones into rocks he would feel next, but the bite of a bullet burning into flesh.

But the shot never came.

The marshal hit the rocks with a thud that pumped the breath from his body, gasped, winced, struggled to turn in time to see Rosen's wide eyes rolling in his head, his mouth sag open and the blood began to bubble at his lips. It was not until Rosen spun round slowly that Keetch saw the blade buried deep in his neck.

Beyond him, his shape shimmering against the light, stood the figure of McKee, his flat, steady gaze as uncompromising as the glare.

★　★　★

'That was close — too damned close,' winced Keetch, scuttling through the rocks with McKee to where Charlie, Doc and the sheriff waited at a distance. 'But thanks,' he added.

McKee merely grunted a response, slowed the pace and finally paused to listen, urging the marshal to his side. 'Darringo's closer than we reckoned,' he murmured, catching the drifting, echoing sounds of voices, horses, shouted orders. 'He'll be plannin' on trappin' us up here and pickin' us off like flies.'

'You figure for that lion track of Charlie's bein' our best shot?'

'That's for Charlie to decide. Let's move.'

Charlie was in no doubt. 'The track's still our best chance,' he judged. 'With Johnny Rosen no longer an ace in his pack, Darringo will be lookin' now to leave nobody standin', and that mebbe includes the Montana rancher himself. But he's goin' to have to look to his own salvation.'

Doc Whipple sighed and ran a tired hand over his tired face. 'Hell, this ain't no place for men of our age, Charlie Roy. Still, I guess you might say you got your man, Marshal. Johnny Rosen ain't goin' to be no loss to nobody.'

'McKee got my man,' said Keetch,

rubbing a hand across his bruised chest. 'And I hope you recovered the knife, mister.'

McKee tapped the handle at his belt, and winked.

'It was Rosen got us out here in the first place,' mused Charlie, 'but he ain't goin' to be one spit of a help gettin' us out.'

'Is anybody?' frowned Doc.

The men were silent for a moment as the sounds of the *bandidos* drifted from the rocks and parched scrub below the grey sprawl of the tor.

'Is it my imagination or does there seem to be more of them down there?' wondered the sheriff.

'There's more, you can bet to that,' said Keetch. 'And they're fast surroundin' us. That I can vouch for. Seen 'em with my own eyes.'

Charlie settled his hat firmly on his head. 'Then let's go see if we're any good at bein' mountain lions.'

24

The lion track was little more than the width of a man's boot in places, less in others, and sometimes non-existent where it broke between jagged crags on its descent to the lower rocks and scrubland.

'Hell,' groaned Doc, 'don't know how a lion made it, never mind a man tacklin' it.'

'The drop's sheer in some parts, so you're goin' to have to watch your step,' said Charlie, peering hard at the prospect.

'You can say that again,' agreed the sheriff.

'Never mind your step, it's our backs we need to watch right now,' urged McKee, gesturing anxiously for the others to take cover. 'We got company. Darringo's men.'

'Hell,' groaned Doc again, 'if it ain't

one thing, it's the darned other!'

The men slid like shadows to whatever cover they could find among the scatterings of boulders as the figures of the advancing *bandidos* took shape against the glare and shimmer.

Sheriff Grove drew Doc to his side. 'Stay close,' he grunted. 'And handle that piece like you mean it. We're talkin' life and death here.'

'No shootin' til we've got proper targets,' hissed the marshal. 'Don't waste lead — it's in short supply!'

Charlie blinked on the now fierce light and thought affectionately for a moment of the veranda and his rocker at the clapboard house back home. 'Should've stayed right there,' he grumbled to himself. He spat resentfully and settled to watch.

McKee had slid a distance to his left and eased into the comparative cool of the shade of an untidy outcrop. His gaze narrowed on the figures still scurrying across the tor like flies at a carcass. He counted six, then eight, maybe ten, and there could be more behind them.

'We're fast bein' outnumbered,' called Keetch.

'And outflanked,' added Doc, glancing anxiously behind him at the lion track and the sheer drop. 'Cold comfort there,' he muttered.

McKee drew the knife from his belt and felt for the bulk of the reserve in the folds of his shirt. He was going to have to make the throwing of them his best yet. No hesitation, no missing . . .

A ghostly silence settled over the tor as the *bandidos* finally dropped from sight behind their cover.

'They know we're here,' whispered Doc at the sheriff's side.

'You bet they do,' said Grove, blinking on the sweat at his eyes. 'They're waitin' on orders.'

'Now's the time for some smart thinkin'.'

'Clean out of it!' grunted Grove.

Charlie dismissed his thoughts of the rocker, but not before resolving he would never leave it again should he make it home — excepting, of course, for a daily visit to Smoky O'Mara's bar.

Marshal Keetch tensed, conscious of where McKee had positioned himself. 'See anythin'?' he asked, in a voice that had dried to a dead creek bed.

'Nothin', answered McKee, 'but I've got some of 'em fixed. Hard to say for certain how many there are.'

'Too damned many!'

They continued to wait and watch, three, five, close on ten minutes before a movement concentrated their attention and focused their eyes on the sudden bulk of Darringo straddled atop a boulder just out of gunshot range.

'Hey, gringos,' shouted the bandit leader, his teeth flashing, the sweat already glistening on his face, 'so what's with all this trouble you're giving me? What's your problem, eh? You turn my horses loose — and it was not so easy rounding them up — you kill my men, and then, Heaven above preserve us, you get to knifing my good friend

Johnny Rosen. Now, what you want to go doing that for, eh? That blade man you've got there is very dangerous. Something must be done about him.'

Darringo erupted in a fit of laughter and growls that set his vast gut rolling at his waist like a surging high tide.

'We could mebbe hit him from here,' said Grove.

'No,' urged Keetch. 'Not yet. One shot and all hell will break out.'

'So, gringos, what to do, eh?' Darringo began again. 'You can't go back — not even you would risk that track, surely. You goin' to make a fight of it and let my men kill you all? Such a waste. Come forward, give yourselves up. You have Darringo's word of honour that you will be treated fairly, even the man with the blade, although he may have to answer to Johnny's father for the death of his son.'

He paused, made a soft gesture to someone hidden to his left, another to the right.

Doc spat. 'Man's word ain't worth

dirt,' he mouthed.

Keetch's eyes narrowed on Darringo's gestures. 'He's makin' to close in,' he hissed to McKee.

Charlie took a firmer grip on the already sticky handle of the Colt in his right hand. Sheriff Grove levelled his Winchester.

'You decided, gringos?' shouted Darringo, relaxing his weight to one hip. 'We do not have all day. Time is pressing and I have other matters to attend to.'

'Tell him, Marshal,' said Grove. 'Tell him what he can do with his offer.'

Keetch cleared his throat. 'Best get to doin' what you've got to do,' he called. 'We ain't for shiftin'.'

Darringo sneered, growled, spat violently, and waved to the hidden men as he slid away from the boulder.

And within seconds the grey, haunted tor was echoing to the blaze and roar of gunfire.

* * *

'Cover me,' yelled McKee above the whining, crackling din.

'What's your plan?' winced Keetch, ducking at the scream of rifle shots passing over him.

McKee squirmed closer to the marshal's cover. 'Way I see it, we've got only one: eliminate Darringo.'

'Sonofa-goddamn-bitch, that's some tall order, mister, specially now.' Keetch ducked again at another scorching scream of firing from the hidden *bandidos*. 'And how you proposin' to do that?'

'Get to him. Is there any other way?' McKee risked a quick glance into the firing. 'He's back there somewhere directin' his men, givin' his orders. If he can be taken out, there's a chance the rats might call it a day.'

'Hope and a prayer reckonin', but it's got to be worth a try. I'll be backin' you close as I can get.'

'Give me two minutes' start, then let the lead rip and follow on. Can you warn the others?'

'Do my best,' said Keetch. 'You get movin'.'

McKee waited only seconds to take a deep breath, lick the sweat clear of his lips, gather his senses, then shift like a sidewinder heading for shade.

'What's goin' on?' hissed Doc to Sheriff Grove. 'McKee and Keetch still with us?'

'Hang on, the marshal's signallin',' frowned Grove, trying to fix his gaze between the volleys of fire. He waited, watching, ducking. 'McKee's movin',' he said at last. 'Keetch is goin' with him. He wants all the cover we can summon.'

'I'd figure for McKee goin' for Darringo,' muttered Doc. 'That'd be his thinkin'.'

'I'll go warn Charlie, then we'll get busy.'

McKee squirmed on, his knife tight in his grip, his legs, arms and body working frantically to keep him moving forwards through the cover of rocks above the line of fire, the grit and dirt scraping mercilessly at his flesh. He paused to listen to the blaze of the returned fire. Hell, he wondered, how long before the sheriff, Doc, Charlie and Keetch ran out of ammunition?

Another yard, the sweat clouding his vision; another painful squirm . . . The heel of the boot crashed across the knuckles of his left hand like an avalanche.

He gasped, winced, and stared into the leering face of a swarthy *bandido*, his rifle already levelling for a point-blank shot.

McKee's right hand gripping the knife lunged at the man's leg, burying the blade deep in his calf. The *bandido* screamed, but the sound was lost on the gunfire and the sudden blaze at McKee's back of the marshal's Winchester.

McKee turned briefly, grinned and acknowledged Keetch's cover, then retrieved the knife from the dead *bandido*'s leg and squirmed on.

The gunfire blazed again. McKee

risked another backward glance. No sign now of Keetch. Nothing of the others. He blinked on the swirls of smoke and cordite, wiped the sweat from his face, waited, and came carefully, steadily to his knees, then to a crouching position.

He could see Darringo only yards ahead.

His grip on the knife began to tingle. He relaxed, swallowed, heard the boom of the bandit leader's voice as if it came to him down a long, empty tunnel. The grip tightened. He shifted a boot, stood taller.

Damn! Darringo was turning.

'The man with the knife,' he scoffed, on a flash of white teeth. 'You are very persistent, gringo. Too persistent perhaps.'

The flashing smile faded. McKee's gaze steadied, watching the hand that rested only inches from the butt of the Colt at Darringo's waist.

'You have been a troublesome problem, gringo,' he boomed again above the crack and roar of the continuing gunfire. 'And you are costly. I lose men, horses, time. I cannot afford to let you live!'

Darringo's hand moved. The fingers were on the butt, closing like anxious claws. The man's eyes gleamed, the white teeth flashed, sweat beaded like rain, the voice boomed and bellowed through a laughter that rocked the body as if an avalanche rumbled in its gut.

But the blade had already left McKee's hand, its flight smooth and steady, the aim deadly.

Darringo's eyes widened and bulged, his bulk stumbling forward like a dislodged boulder under the momentum of a slope. He drew the Colt, tried to level it, lost his grip as the body weakened, the blood flowing freely now from where the blade lay deep in dark flesh.

He groaned as he hit the ground with a shuddering thud. A last breath hissed from his mouth, and then he was suddenly dead and no more.

Two *bandidos* watching at a distance exchanged quick glances, shouted to others nearby and turned to head into the haunted light and back across the tor.

★ ★ ★

'Not one,' announced Marshal Keetch an hour later, his gaze ranging slowly over the sunlit rocks. 'They've gone, every last one of the rats. Haven't even bothered to take the body of Darringo with them. So much for loyalty.'

'I ain't complainin',' said Doc, running a bandanna across the sticky band of his hat. 'I'm just grateful to McKee here and that knack of his with a blade. Say this for you, fella, that's one helluva skill to acquire!'

'You can say that again,' agreed Sheriff Grove. He mopped his brow. 'Somehow don't seem real, does it? All that — the dead men, the losses, the sheer darned effort of it all — and then this: just silence.'

Charlie Roy came wearily to his feet from the rocks. 'Yeah,' he sighed, 'and a long ways back to Red Creeks. And, I might remind you, no horses to get us there.'

'Hell,' moaned Keetch, 'that's goin' to be one helluva walk home!'

'Mebbe not,' murmured McKee. 'Look what's crossin' the tor.'

The men turned to shield their gazes on the approaching figure of Edgar Rosen leading a team of horses.

'I got lucky,' called the rancher. 'I stayed alive. Don't ask me how, I just did. So I put myself to good use: rounded up these mounts and hid away with them while Darringo's men were otherwise occupied.' He halted. 'Never doubted you'd come through,' he smiled, glancing at McKee.

'Well, we're sure as hell glad you did what you did,' began Grove, 'but what about — '

'That son of mine?' said Rosen. 'He's stayin' right where he lies. I've already covered his body with rocks. He don't warrant more by my reckonin'. He made his choice . . . Meantime, Montana beckons. There's work to be done, a life to be lived. And you fellas will get your fees as promised. I'll wire them through to your nearest banks.' He smiled and offered the clutch of reins. 'And now, gentlemen, your horses await!'

It was early evening with the sky still high and a warm breeze blowing easy across the open plain, when Charlie drew his mount alongside McKee.

'Ain't sorry to see the last of them mountains and no mistake,' he murmured. 'It's that rocker and veranda for me, mister. The scoutin' days are over. And you, McKee, what you plannin'?'

'Oh, I guess I'll just keep driftin',' smiled McKee. 'Seems to be in my nature. But I'll be back at Red Creeks one day. You bet to it.'

'Don't doubt it. I'll be watchin'. Rockin' and watchin'. Just don't leave it too long, *gringo*!'